MURDER AT THE PET BOUTIQUE

WAGGING TAIL COZY MYSTERY SERIES

CINDY BELL

CONTENTS

Cover Design by Annie Moril

ISBN: 9781728777115

CHAPTER 1

It was just after nine in the morning, and the town of Dahlia was bustling. Nikki had found her way to the newest shop in town, *Dahlia's Pet Boutique,* a pet supplies and gift shop. There were still 'Grand Opening' signs in the window, but the shop had been open for almost a month. As a dog walker, pet sitter, and general lover of animals, Nikki was drawn to the new shop. But she wasn't there just to check it out. She was on a mission. One of her favorite clients, Mrs. Whitter, had decided to throw a birthday party for her Chihuahua, Princess. With the party planned for Saturday, Nikki simply had to find the perfect gift. Mrs. Whitter was one of the wealthiest people in town, and although Nikki knew she would appreciate any gift, she wanted to try and impress her.

There were ample clothing choices. All of them served a purpose of either protecting the animals from the sun or keeping them warm. Nikki noticed that several of the pieces had fake gems sewn into them, but only in places that the dog wouldn't be able to get to them and chew them free. She liked that the designer was safety-minded. She moved on from the clothing, past the toys and bedding, to the 'Puppy and Me' section. It contained items for dogs that matched with items that could be worn by their owners.

As Nikki sorted through the collars, she noticed that some were sold in sets with matching key rings. The collars were a solid color, with decorative designs swirled through them. The key rings were silver paw prints, with a jewel the same color as the collar in the center. Clearly the jewel was fake, but it was still pretty. She knew that Mrs. Whitter's favorite color was green. She decided to search for a green set.

Then Mrs. Whitter and Princess can match. Nikki smiled to herself at the thought. She was sure that Mrs. Whitter would like that idea.

As Nikki brushed back her wavy, light brown

hair, she peered at each collar on the rack. She found a green collar that was perfect for Princess' tiny size, but there was no matching green key ring. There were blue key rings, and yellow ones, even pink ones, but no green. Determined to get the special gift she turned her attention to the front counter.

Behind it the owner of the shop appeared to be busy packing items into boxes.

"Hi Bryan." Nikki smiled as she walked up to the counter with the green collar in her hand. "Do you have the matching key ring that goes with this set? I'd really like to buy it."

"No, I'm sorry. We're out of the green." He turned back towards the boxes that lined a shelf behind the counter.

As she watched, he dropped a key ring with a green gem into the box.

"Well, what about that one?" Nikki smiled as she pointed it out. "That looks like it would match. I'll take it."

"No, I'm sorry, these aren't for sale." Bryan closed the lid of the box.

"Even if I paid a little extra?" She frowned as she reached into her purse for her wallet.

"No." His tone became firmer as he turned

around to face her. He met her eyes. "Like I said, these aren't available for purchase."

"Okay." Nikki took a step back from the counter, annoyed. She'd finally found the perfect gift for Princess, and Bryan couldn't be bothered to let her have just one key ring. She decided that she would shop elsewhere. Normally, Bryan was such a friendly and funny man. He always wore a bright smile and was eager to talk about his latest creations. But today it seemed as if he couldn't get her out of the shop fast enough. Maybe he was just having a rough day, but it bothered her. She didn't want to give her business to someone that didn't appreciate it.

With one more look in the direction of the perfect green collar, Nikki walked towards the door. Before she could reach it, it swung open. A woman who looked to be in her twenties pushed her way past her. The collision was harmless, but the attitude of the woman made Nikki pause and watch her.

"You!" The woman shouted and pointed at Bryan. "You almost killed me! Are you insane?"

Drawn in by the intensity of the moment, Nikki continued to linger near the door. She watched as Bryan turned to face the woman. His cheeks burned crimson in reaction to the woman's accusation.

"I didn't kill you, did I?"

"And I'm supposed to feel grateful for that?" She snapped at him. "You were driving like a mad man! You should lose your license before you do kill someone!"

"It was a mistake, you're fine, I think it's best if we just move on." Bryan crossed his arms as he studied her. "Are you going to leave my shop, or do I need to call the police?"

"Oh, go ahead and call them. I'm sure they would love to hear all about you hitting me, and then taking off."

"You were fine!" He shouted, then started to step around the counter. "I didn't see the need to call the police over something as trivial as a fender bender."

"A fender bender that could have taken my life." She shook her head as she glared at him. "One day soon, buddy someone is going to show you what it's like to face your own death, and then you will have an idea of what you put me through. Very soon!" She turned and pushed past Nikki again to get back out of the shop.

Nikki stared after her, curious about the details of the woman's encounter with Bryan. When she glanced back at him, he had already stepped back behind the counter. His back was to her, as he continued to pack boxes. Whatever had happened between him and the woman, he didn't seem terribly concerned about it. However, the woman's words echoed through Nikki's mind. Clearly, she had been traumatized by the accident, and she had a lot of anger towards Bryan. But that didn't give her the right to threaten him. Nikki stepped out through the door of the shop and did her best to shake off the experience. She didn't want it to ruin the rest of her day.

As Nikki tried to get back into a positive mindset she wondered where she would find a gift for Princess. As one of her favorite clients, she wanted to make sure that both Mrs. Whitter and Princess knew how much she valued them. However, her dog walker and pet sitting salary was modest at best, and she always had to keep her budget in mind. Luckily, Dahlia had quite a few shops to choose from. Most were individual businesses, and many featured local artists, and designers. The shops were packed full of unique creations. As she started down the street towards the next row of shops, she heard a motorcycle roar to life. It bolted out from behind a building, and right past her, so loud that she winced.

As Nikki continued down the sidewalk she paused to look through the window of one of the shops. There were several different pairs of boots, as well as purses to match. She looked them over without much interest. Several of her friends insisted the shop sold the latest and hottest designs in footwear. She tried to blend in by pretending to be interested, but she still didn't understand why it mattered so much what she wore on her feet. Now, if they were little puppy boots, she might feel differently. She laughed a little as she continued on to the next shop. Large paintings filled the front window. She knew that the artist who owned the shop offered to create custom paintings for people off a photograph, but she doubted that could be done in the two days before the party. She was also fairly certain it would be out of her price range.

As Nikki moved on to the next shop, she waved to a few familiar people across the street. She'd grown up in Dahlia, and knew most of the people that lived there. It made her feel fairly secure as she strolled along the sidewalk. The next shop featured an assortment of gifts in the window. She decided to step in and take a look. Maybe her gift would be more for Mrs. Whitter.

As Nikki browsed, the owner of the shop sat

behind the counter with a magazine in her hands. Nellie Cooper had owned *Cooper's Gifts and More* for at least ten years. However, she never kept the same products in her shop for longer than a few months. The variety made a trip to her shop a treasure hunt, every time. As Nikki wandered through the shelves and looked over each item, several things seemed good enough, but nothing was that one perfect gift. After a few more minutes, she waved goodbye to Nellie, and headed back outside. A little frustrated with her shopping trip, she decided to stop at the café that her friend Gina owned. Their conversations always left her feeling good. As she pushed the door open and stepped inside, she noticed that the café was fairly empty. She must have missed the breakfast rush.

"Hi Nikki." Gina smiled from behind the counter. "I just made some fresh coffee, want a cup?"

"Sure, thanks." Nikki smiled as she took a stool at the counter. "And some rye toast, please. I had a big group of dogs for the early morning walk, so I didn't have time for breakfast."

"Mm, good choice." Gina winked at her as she turned to pour the coffee. "How is your morning going?"

"It would be better if I could find a gift for Princess' birthday." Nikki sighed, then smiled as she accepted the cup of coffee. "Thanks."

"Ah yes, the elusive perfect gift for a canine." Gina raised an eyebrow. "A bone comes to mind?"

"Are you kidding?" Nikki laughed and shook her head. "Mrs. Whitter has Princess on such a special diet, she would never dream of letting her have a bone, or any other treats that aren't on her approved list."

"Wow!" Gina grinned. "Never mind about the bone then. I'll be right back with your toast, hon." She disappeared into the kitchen.

Nikki stirred some cream into her coffee and savored the aroma that wafted up from the hot liquid. As moments slipped by, she began to relax. It was a little silly to be so wound up over a gift for a dog, she realized that. She knew that Mrs. Whitter would appreciate anything that she gave her.

"So, what kind of gift are you looking for? Maybe I can help you figure something out." Gina set down Nikki's plate of toast in front of her.

"I thought I'd found the perfect gift." Nikki frowned as she recounted her experience with Bryan that morning. "Usually he's such a nice guy, at least the times I've interacted with him before, he has been."

"I agree. I really like his ideas, and the colors he uses in his designs. It's strange that he wouldn't sell you the key ring. But that isn't the only strange behavior he's had lately."

"It isn't?" Nikki took a bite of her toast, then met Gina's eyes.

"No, he was in here the other day, and I actually had to ask him and another man to leave." She leaned against the counter and lowered her voice. "Bryan was in here with Royce Blake. Do you know Royce?"

"No, I don't think so." Nikki took another bite of her toast, her interest piqued.

"He's fairly new to town. He's trying to get his business off the ground. He's confided in me a few times over his morning coffee. Anyway, everything seemed to be fine at first, then all of a sudden the two were arguing. It got so heated that I had to ask them both to leave. Honestly, I thought I was going to have to call the police."

"What were they arguing about?" Nikki tried to picture Bryan being so irate that Gina had to ask him to leave. The man was usually cheerful, if not a bit over the top with his joy. What could upset him so much?

"From what I could gather, it had to do with the shop. I guess somehow Bryan stole the rental space out from under Royce. At least, that was how Royce saw it. But that's not what made it come close to blows. It got personal. Royce said something about Bryan's brother, I don't know exactly what, but that's when Bryan really lost it. It was terrible." She frowned. "I was glad when they both left."

"Do you know Bryan's brother?" Nikki raised an eyebrow.

"No, I didn't even know he had one. You know Bryan doesn't live in town, he just runs his shop here. It's only been about a month since he opened. I haven't gotten to know him that well." Gina shrugged as she grabbed the coffee pot. When she freshened up Nikki's coffee, she glanced past her towards two men that walked into the café. "Oops excuse me, I actually have work to do." She winked at Nikki, then walked off to greet the two men.

As Nikki finished her toast she wondered if Bryan might be in some kind of trouble. It sounded like his temper had gotten short, and his personality had changed quite a bit. She left a nice tip for Gina, along with payment for her meal, then headed to the door. As she walked past the two men who had just been seated, she heard a snippet of their conversation.

"If he knows what's good for him, then he'll fall in line. If not, then we'll have to take care of the problem."

Nikki glanced in the direction of the men, as she thought the comment was a little unusual. One was older, perhaps in his forties, he had short, curly, dark brown hair that was receding slightly, and he wore a sleek trench coat. The other looked to be in his twenties, around her age, he had blond hair that fell over his eyes, and he wore a motorcycle jacket. The younger man caught her eye, and she realized that her attention had been spotted. She glanced away and hurried towards the door. It was just about time to take Princess for her walk. She was almost out the door, when a shoulder brushed against hers. She looked up, and spotted Quinn. Or Detective Quinn Grant, she reminded herself.

"Hi there." He smiled, an expression that showed off the dimples she'd fallen in love with when she was just a teen. Before their paths had crossed again, she thought she'd never see him again. Now it seemed she was always running into him.

"Hi." She stepped through the door as she realized he couldn't get past.

"What are you up to today?" He stepped back through the door as well.

"Oh, just shopping for Princess' birthday party." Nikki smiled as she met his eyes.

"I'm sorry, a dog is having a birthday party?" Quinn laughed. "You're not serious, are you?"

"I sure am. Princess is like Mrs. Whitter's baby." She shrugged. "Many people have pets they feel that way about."

"You're right, I guess I've just never been that attached to an animal before." He held her gaze. "It's sweet, really."

"You should come." The words jumped out of Nikki's mouth. After she spoke them, she had no idea why she did. Of course, Quinn wouldn't be interested in attending a dog's birthday party.

"You don't think Mrs. Whitter would mind?" Quinn crossed his arms. "I wasn't exactly invited."

"No, she wouldn't mind at all. She'd love to see you." Nikki's heartbeat quickened as she realized he was actually interested. "It's Saturday, at one."

"Sure, I'll be there." He smiled again. "Too bad we missed each other for breakfast."

"Yes, too bad." Nikki was tempted to claim she

hadn't eaten yet, but she didn't want to be late for Princess. "Enjoy your meal."

"Thanks." He opened the door to the café and stepped through it.

Nikki lingered for just a moment outside the door. Nothing had changed. Each time she saw him, all of those old feelings she had for him were stirred. But that didn't matter. It had been a high school crush, and it had never been mutual. To distract herself, she began to head in the direction of Mrs. Whitter's house.

CHAPTER 2

Nikki only walked Princess when Mrs. Whitter had something to do and couldn't take her herself. Princess was such a tiny dog that Mrs. Whitter preferred to have her walked alone. Nikki didn't mind as she loved her time with Princess. As she walked towards Mrs. Whitter's house she noticed the shift from single family homes with neat, square lawns and bay windows, to sprawling mansions and acres of property. The high, stone walls and wrought iron gates that guarded these wealthy homes blended with the greenery of Dahlia quite well, but the message was clear. There were two sides of Dahlia, and they rarely blended. However, Nikki was immune to that as she walked several dogs in the neighborhood.

When Nikki reached Mrs. Whitter's property she noticed an unfamiliar car parked at the end of her long drive. She stared at it for a moment as she tried to piece together who might be there for a visit. She didn't want to interrupt, but she was already a few minutes late. She knocked lightly on the front door, and waited for a response. She could hear voices inside, Mrs. Whitter's and a man's. It was too muffled for her to recognize. Quick fear bolted through her. Mrs. Whitter was very vulnerable as she lived alone, and she was very well-off. What if whoever was inside intended to do her harm? Nikki pushed the door open and stepped inside.

"Mrs. Whitter?"

"In the living room, Nikki!" Mrs. Whitter called out, her voice tight.

Nikki knew that voice well. It usually meant that Mrs. Whitter was annoyed about something. She could be a demanding woman when she wanted something a certain way, and quite stubborn when anyone challenged her. Nikki followed her voice into the living room, and was surprised to see Bryan there. Mrs. Whitter held Princess in her arms as she faced off with the much larger man.

"I just don't understand why you sold it to me in the first place."

"I'm very sorry, Mrs. Whitter, it was a terrible mistake. But I must have the collar back." His eyebrows pinched together as his cheeks flushed.

"I'm very sorry as well, Bryan, but I will not be giving the collar back." Mrs. Whitter huffed as she did her best to cover Princess' ears. "It is a very special gift for Princess' birthday, and her party is only two days away. Now, I made the purchase fair and square, I would not like to discuss this any further." She stroked the top of Princess' head.

The dog wagged her tail eagerly at the sight of Nikki.

"What's going on here? Is everything okay?" Nikki crossed her arms as she looked at Bryan. After what she'd just heard from Gina about him, she didn't trust him to be calm or stable.

"I'm simply trying to explain to Mrs. Whitter that the collar I sold her is unsafe." Bryan frowned as he looked over at Nikki. "I received a call from one of my customers who bought the jeweled collar. The color ran into the dog's fur when it rained and stained it. I wouldn't want that to happen to Princess. I'm doing my best to make sure that anyone who bought one of these collars returns them." He turned his attention back to Mrs. Whitter. "And I can assure you, Mrs. Whitter, I will more than make up for the inconvenience. I will personally craft you a custom collar for Princess, that you will both love. Please, I don't want Princess' fur to be stained."

"I understand." Mrs. Whitter sighed as she lowered her eyes. "I wouldn't ever want for that to happen to my baby." She gave the dog a soft snuggle. "It is too bad though, it was so beautiful, and our favorite color."

"Again, I'm very sorry." Bryan wiped at his brow, where beads of sweat had gathered. "Do you have the collar?"

"Yes, yes, I'll get it for you." Mrs. Whitter frowned as she handed Princess over to Nikki. "Sorry for the delay, Nikki, just let me handle this then you and Princess can take your walk."

"It's no problem, Mrs. Whitter." Nikki smiled as Princess settled in her arms. The little dog stretched her head up to lick Nikki's cheeks.

"Aw, she loves kisses." Mrs. Whitter giggled, then headed down the hallway.

Now that Nikki knew Mrs. Whitter had bought Princess a collar for her birthday, she was relieved she hadn't been able to buy the collar and key ring set.

Alone with Bryan, Nikki noticed that he fidgeted with the hem of his button-down shirt. He was just about as round as he was tall, which could make for an intimidating person, but his boisterous personality usually put her at ease. Unfortunately, she didn't see much of that personality today.

"Are you okay, Bryan?"

"I'm fine, thanks." He glanced at her. "I just have a lot to do."

"I understand." She watched him as Mrs. Whitter returned with a small, black box. Perhaps that was why he wouldn't sell her the key ring, he'd found out they were faulty as well. But then why had he boxed them up in individual boxes? Where was he sending them?

"Here you are." Mrs. Whitter held out the box to him.

"Thank you." He took the box and flipped it open. "I will make this up to you, Mrs. Whitter, I promise."

"It better be something spectacular, and by Saturday!" Mrs. Whitter pursed her lips.

Nikki caught a glimpse of the collar just before Bryan closed the box. She noticed that although it was a different design, it had the same green stones as the key ring Nikki wanted to buy Mrs. Whitter. That didn't surprise her, since Mrs. Whitter adored anything and everything green.

"It will be, I promise." He gave her a quick smile, wiped his brow, then nodded to Nikki on his way out.

Nikki wondered if he was worried because he might be in some legal trouble due to the recall.

"It's a good thing Princess is safe, you wouldn't want her fur to be bright green." Nikki stroked the dog's fur. "You made the right decision, Mrs. Whitter."

"Oh yes, I know. It's just so disappointing. I'm trying to make sure everything is just perfect, and now this is one more thing I have to figure out." She placed her hands on her hips. "Next year, I'm hiring a party planner."

"Is there anything I can help you with?" Nikki looked Mrs. Whitter over. Though she was a short and frail woman, at times she packed a level of strength that Nikki had never seen in another person. She had to be careful not to offend her by treating her too gently, that was a lesson she learned not long after she began pet sitting Princess. She had emphatically explained to Nikki, that she was far tougher than she looked.

"It's okay, I'm sure I can handle it. But thank you for offering." Mrs. Whitter eyed Princess for a moment. "In fact, what would help the most is if you took her for her walk now, so I can get a few things done. I'm pretty sure she's getting suspicious."

"Uh oh." Nikki grinned. "Sure, I'll keep her out a little longer, too."

"Thanks, but not too long, I don't want her getting too much sun. Oh, and make sure you take a bottle of water from the fridge, halfway through the walk have her drink. These warm days worry me." Mrs. Whitter frowned.

"Don't worry, I'll take good care of her." Nikki clipped Princess' leash on her collar, then grabbed the water out of the kitchen. As she headed out through the back door, Princess took a wild leap of delight. She was quite a bold and energetic dog.

"Wait for me, Princess!" Nikki laughed as she broke into a jog. Princess loved to run.

Not long into their walk, Nikki realized that the sun really was a bit intense. She steered Princess towards Pooch Park, so that she could walk on the shaded sidewalk. Nikki was about to give Princess some water, when the sound of shrill sirens made Nikki jump. Dahlia tended to be a quiet place. Loud noises commanded attention. A police car sped past her. One police car wasn't too unusual. But when it was followed by two more, her heart jumped into her throat. What could be happening that warranted that kind of response?

Princess barked and hopped back and forth. She was too distracted to drink the water that Nikki offered her. When an ambulance flashed by, followed by two more police cars, Nikki began to worry. Dahlia didn't have a huge police force. If she were to guess, the entire force might be headed in one direction. Too curious and concerned not to find out what it was all about, she walked Princess in the direction the police cars were headed. She noticed that they stopped outside Bryan's shop. Her eyes widened at the sight of all of the police cars gathered around the small shop. It seemed to her that nothing could be so bad to require such a turn out.

Nikki lingered quite close to the shop. A few minutes later, a stretcher rolled out of the shop. Her heart skipped a beat as she wondered if she might have missed the signs of a heart attack when Bryan was at Mrs. Whitter's house. He had been sweating a bit and seemed nervous. She assumed that he was just acting strangely, but perhaps he was having a medical emergency, and she didn't notice. She could tell that it was him on the stretcher, but it wasn't a heart attack that caused his emergency. She could see the blood-soaked gauze pressed against his chest. Her heart lurched as she realized that he might have been shot. With her eyes wide, she could barely convince herself to take a breath. She had just seen him not even an hour before. As Nikki watched the ambulance drive away, she noticed an officer headed in her direction. She tightened her grip on Princess' leash, and wondered if the officer might scold her for spying.

"Ma'am?" The officer held a notepad in one hand, and had his other hand on his hip. "How long have you been standing here?"

"Not long." Nikki frowned as she looked down at Princess. The dog lunged at the officer, determined to get a sniff of his shoe, but Nikki kept her leash tight and short. "I'm sorry, we'll be on our way."

"It's no trouble, I'd just like to ask you a few questions." He met her eyes and offered a friendly smile. He looked familiar, but she didn't know him by name. She hadn't had much reason to deal directly with the police, but they often patrolled local events.

"Sure, but I'm not sure if I can help." Nikki shrugged.

"Did you happen to hear anything, or see anything?" He opened his notepad and prepared to take a few notes. "And could I have your name?"

"I didn't see or hear anything, I'm sorry." Nikki frowned as she offered her name. "I just followed all of the police cars because I was curious. I have no idea what happened. But is Bryan okay?"

"Did you know him?" His eyes narrowed some as he studied her.

"Not well no. I did go to his shop a few times and see him around town." She noticed that he spoke in the past tense. "What happened to him? It looked like he was shot."

"I can't share too much information, Nikki, but I'm afraid he didn't make it. If you can keep that to yourself until we inform the family, I would appreciate it." The officer locked his eyes to hers.

"Yes, of course I will. How terrible." Nikki pressed her hand against her chest. "How could this happen?"

"That's what we're trying to figure out. So, if you have any information, if you can think of anything at all that might help the investigation, please let us know." He offered her a card.

"Thanks." She took the card. "If I think of anything I'll contact you right away."

"I'm going to ask you to move along. We're going to clear this entire area for the investigation." The officer glanced up and down the street beyond her. "Hopefully, someone saw something."

"Good luck with your investigation." Nikki guided Princess back in the direction of Mrs. Whitter's house. It left her unsettled to think that someone could have been murdered while she was walking Princess. What if she'd gotten to the shop a little sooner? Would she have seen something? Would she have been able to help in some way?

With her stomach in knots she walked up to the front door of Mrs. Whitter's house and knocked lightly on it.

"Nikki, you're back so soon?" Mrs. Whitter frowned as she opened the door. "I thought you were going to keep her out a bit longer."

"I'm sorry, Mrs. Whitter, I forgot." Her cheeks flushed. "Something terrible happened and I didn't think, I just thought it would be best to get Princess home to you."

"What is it? What happened?" Her eyes

widened as she opened the door all the way and gazed at Nikki.

"Bryan has been killed." She shivered as she spoke the words.

"What? Are you certain?" Mrs. Whitter clasped her hand over her mouth as a gentle moan escaped her.

"Yes, I saw him, and I spoke with a police officer. He was killed at his shop." Nikki released Princess from her leash, and the dog raced towards the kitchen. "I can't believe that we just spoke to him a short time ago, and now he's gone."

"Neither can I." Mrs. Whitter tugged at the pearls that hung around her neck. "This is just devastating, absolutely devastating."

"Yes, it is." Nikki grasped her shoulder with a soft touch. "I'm sorry, Mrs. Whitter, are you going to be okay?"

"Yes, of course, I'll be fine. But what am I going to do for a birthday present now?" Mrs. Whitter frowned.

Nikki took a slight step back, startled by Mrs. Whitter's reaction. As the woman wandered off, she muttered about how she needed everything to be perfect.

Nikki stared after her, concerned. Was she so

wrapped up in the party that she didn't realize just how tragic the situation was?

"Mrs. Whitter, please be sure not to tell anyone else. The police haven't had the chance to notify the family, yet." Nikki followed her into the living room.

"Oh right, absolutely. I won't breathe a word about it." She sniffled as she grabbed a tissue from the box on the coffee table. "Bryan." She sighed and wiped at her eyes. "He was a nice man."

"Yes, he was." Nikki met her eyes. "Are you sure you're going to be okay?"

"Yes, I will be. I'm sorry, I just don't know how to react to all of this." She wiped at her eyes again.

"It's okay, Mrs. Whitter." Nikki gave her hand a gentle squeeze. "The police are going to figure out what happened. If you need any help with the party, just let me know."

"I can handle it." Mrs. Whitter sniffed and blinked back her tears. "I'll be fine."

"I know you will be." Nikki squeezed her hand again, then smiled.

"Thank you, Nikki. Princess just loves her walks with you." Mrs. Whitter stood up. "So much to do!"

"I love them, too. Bye, Mrs. Whitter."

Nikki was tempted to offer to help again, but she knew better. Mrs. Whitter did things on her own.

As Nikki left the house she headed in the direction of the next dog she would walk. She had a group of six dogs to collect, and could only hope that their antics would help distract her from the morning's events.

CHAPTER 3

Once Nikki had gathered all of the dogs, she directed them towards the park. It was her favorite place to walk them, as it was free of cars and other dangers. However, getting them not to terrorize the squirrels could be quite a task. For a few minutes she was distracted by their playfulness and joy at being outside. However, it wasn't long before her mind wandered back to Bryan. Who would want to kill him?

Most of the time he was a kind and friendly person. Of course, she didn't know him very well, but from what she did know of him, he didn't seem like someone who would be anyone's target. Had someone tried to rob the shop? Maybe he walked in on it? Guesses and theories rolled through her mind as she attempted to make sense of what happened. When her cell phone rang she jumped in reaction to the sound of her ringtone. She juggled the leashes in her hands and managed to pull her phone out of her pocket. When she saw Quinn's name on the screen, she answered it right away. However, just as she hit the button to accept the call, Coco and Sassy, two of the bigger dogs she walked, lunged for a squirrel. She gasped and almost dropped her phone as she tried to keep control of the dogs.

"Coco, Sassy, you know better!" She huffed as she brought them back to her side, then managed to get the phone between her shoulder and her ear. "Hello?"

"Are you okay?" Quinn's voice greeted her with concern.

"Oh yes, sorry, it's just I'm walking the dogs and Coco and Sassy saw a squirrel." She laughed.

"Ah, those pesky squirrels." Quinn chuckled. "Listen, I'm calling because your name came up in a homicide investigation."

"Yes, I spoke to one of the officers this morning." Nikki kept the leashes tight in her hand.

"Would you mind coming in to talk about it?" Quinn cleared his throat. "I need to comb through what's been done already and make sure nothing was missed."

"I don't mind, but I can't really help. I didn't see anything, like I told the officer. I followed them to the crime scene out of curiosity, but I didn't see or hear anything. I was only there after they were." Nikki continued to guide the dogs along through the park.

"I understand, but I'd still like to speak to you again if that's possible, just to keep the record clear. Is that okay with you?" He spoke in a professional tone.

"Sure, if you think it will help." Nikki noticed the way he spoke to her. She guessed that he was under a good bit of pressure as a young detective, and he needed to make sure everything was accurate.

"I think it would. Thanks, Nikki."

"I just have to take the dogs home. I'll need about an hour?"

"Sure, no rush. I'll be here most of the day. You can text me when you're on your way if you'd like. Thanks again." He hung up the phone.

A little surprised that Quinn hung up so fast, Nikki tucked her phone back into her pocket. She never minded spending some time with him, but she wished she had more to offer to help him with the investigation.

Nikki dropped the dogs at their homes one by one. Coco was the last dog she had to drop off. As she walked him towards his house, she had to pass the pet boutique. When she did, she noticed a man across the street. He stood at the edge of the sidewalk and stared hard at the shop, which was still roped off with police tape. She didn't think she had seen him before. The way he looked at the shop made her heart skip a beat. What was he up to? When he noticed her watching, he began to walk away. That made her even more suspicious. She decided to follow him, for just a few minutes. With Coco in the lead she walked across the street. He turned a corner and disappeared inside a real estate agency.

Nikki continued past the agency in the direction of Coco's house. She was sure that there were many reasons for him to be looking at the shop. Just like her, he could have been curious about what happened there. Maybe he was a friend of Bryan's and just wanted to figure out what happened. No matter what, there was no law against spying on crime scenes. If there was, she would have been in a lot of trouble. Once she dropped off Coco she headed back towards the police station. As she did she considered what she knew about Bryan.

Bryan's shop had only been open for about a month. He was generally friendly and eager to meet people. She recalled a few occasions where he'd joked with her, and even asked her advice on some of his designs. He seemed like an open person. So, why would anyone want him dead? Perhaps if he actually lived in Dahlia she would know him a little better. As she neared the police station she recalled the woman who had threatened him that morning. At the time it seemed like a fairly innocent tantrum, but now that Bryan was dead she had to wonder if maybe this woman had something to do with it.

Nikki pulled open the door to the police station and stepped inside. Right away she was hit with the scent of cinnamon. A little surprised to associate that smell with the police station, she followed her nose in the direction of it. It wasn't long before she discovered a tray of freshly baked apple and cinnamon pastries. She smiled to herself as she knew exactly who they came from. Gina must have dropped them off to the police officers. She liked to surprise people with gifts like that.

"Nikki." Quinn called out to her from the door of his office.

She smiled as she caught sight of him. For a moment she recalled what it was like to be a gangling teenager with a hopeless crush. Was she still that gangling teenager in her heart? She did her best to focus on the matter at hand as she walked towards him. Quinn had a career, and he had to prove himself as a detective. She didn't want to do anything to distract him from that.

"It looks like Gina love-bombed the station." Nikki stepped past him, into his office.

"Yes, she did, thankfully. It gave everyone a boost after the events of this morning." He gestured to the chair across from his desk. "I promise I won't keep you long."

"Oh, it's no problem, anything I can do to help, I'm happy to do." As Nikki sat down across from him she hoped he wasn't that eager to send her off. But then, perhaps the connection she still felt between them was just her imagination.

Quinn glanced up at her, met her eyes, then looked back down at the file open on his desk.

"So, it seems that you had some recent contact with Bryan. Is that correct?"

"Yes, some." Nikki cleared her throat. "But I don't know anything about what happened at the shop."

"So you've told me." Quinn looked up at her again, his eyes inquisitive as they searched hers.

"I just don't want to waste your time." Nikki shrugged, then directed her attention to the photographs on the walls of his office. She'd never noticed them before. Had he recently put them up? She recognized some of his family, and one of a familiar place, the section of bay where they'd had their encounter many years ago.

"You could never do that."

"Hmm?" She glanced back at him.

"I just mean, time with you, could never be a waste." Quinn looked back at the file on his desk.

"Thanks." Her cheeks flushed. She stared down at the desk, too.

"Listen, we looked over the surveillance footage from Bryan's shop today. Unfortunately, it was not running the whole morning, but it did capture some stuff before the murder. You're on the recording." He folded his hands on top of the file. "Can you tell me what your interaction was like with Bryan? Did you notice anything out of the ordinary in his behavior?"

"Oh yes, I stopped in to try to find a birthday present for Princess. You know, every other time I've been around Bryan he was always so nice, and talkative. He loved to discuss art, and anything that had to do with animals, so we got along pretty well." Nikki smiled at the memories that trickled through her mind. "But this morning, he was very stand-offish. I wanted to purchase a particular item, it was a key ring with a fake green gem, and he insisted that it was not for sale. He refused to sell it to me, even though he had it right there behind the counter. It wasn't just that he refused to sell it, it was more about how he refused to sell it. He was short, and acted like me being there annoyed him. It was strange."

"I see. Was there anything else he mentioned? Did he say anything about why he was upset?" He picked up a pen and made a note in the file.

"No, he didn't say anything else to me. But then as I was leaving, this other woman came in." Nikki's eyes widened as she recalled the way she behaved. "She started accusing him of trying to kill her. And they argued back and forth a bit. I left after that, though."

"Heather Cantrells." Quinn nodded as he glanced back up at her. "We saw her on the surveillance video as well. Thanks for filling in some of what was said. There was no audio on the recording. We plan to speak to Heather as soon as we can find her. Did she mention what she was upset about?"

"Yes, she did. It was something about an accident, him almost hitting her, or something like that." She shook her head. "I don't know exactly."

"That's all right. That fills in some blanks for us. We were able to identify her from the video, and we did find a record of an accident she reported, so this confirms why she was there, and why she was upset. When we speak to her, hopefully she will be forthcoming with some additional information." Quinn sat back in his chair and wiped a hand across his eyes. "Was there anything else strange about his behavior? Anything at all?"

"Well, when I saw him later at Mrs. Whitter's—"

"Wait," Quinn interrupted, and sat forward at the same time. "You saw him again? At what time?"

"It was just after I left you at the café. I walked to Mrs. Whitter's and I found him inside, speaking to her." Nikki narrowed her eyes. "I think maybe around eleven. Anyway, he was quite nervous. He demanded that she give him back the collar she'd purchased for Princess' birthday. Of course, this upset her, and she didn't want to give it to him. But when he explained it was a safety issue, she gave it back to him."

"What made you think he was nervous?" He made another note in the file. "Thanks, you're filling in the timeline for me."

"He just seemed that way. Again, he wasn't very friendly. He looked agitated. He just kept insisting that she return the collar to him. I know he cares about animals, but it struck me as him being a little overly concerned." She frowned as she looked across the desk at him. "I'm sorry that I don't have more to share with you about it."

"It's actually very helpful." He scribbled down a few things. "I'm surprised he went to Mrs. Whitter's house. I may need to speak with her as well."

"If you do, be prepared. She's already pretty tense about the party, and after what happened to Bryan, she's even more stressed." Nikki winced as she recalled the woman's anxiety. "I offered to help, but she's too stubborn to take it."

"I'll be sure to sweet talk her." Quinn winked lightly at her, then set his pen down. "And you, are you okay?"

"What do you mean?" Nikki met his eyes.

"I mean, you saw this man twice today, and now he's been killed. That has to be a little jarring."

She studied him, curious as to whether he asked the question for personal reasons, or to get an idea of whether she might be a suspect. Could he really consider her one?

"It's still setting in I think." Nikki looked down at her hands, which were splayed open across her lap. "It is upsetting to think about."

"Try not to be too worried. I'm sure that this was a targeted attack which means the public shouldn't be at risk. But it's always good to be cautious." He picked up his pen, again. "Oh, one more question. Did you hear or see a motorcycle nearby the shop around the time of the murder?"

"No, I didn't. Why?" She stared at him with interest.

"A witness recalls hearing a motorcycle nearby. I just thought you might have heard it as well." He tapped the pen against the file.

"No, I'm sorry I didn't. I did hear one near the shops earlier in the morning." She sighed as she looked back down at her hands. "Like I said, I really don't know anything about what happened."

"You've helped quite a bit." Quinn stood up behind his desk. "I'll walk you out."

"You don't have to do that." She stood up as well, and couldn't avoid looking directly into his eyes.

"I don't mind." As he opened the office door for

her, he brushed his hand lightly along the curve of her back.

Nikki felt like she had butterflies in her stomach. There it was again, that chemistry that always seemed to be there. Too bad it appeared to be one-sided. As a sensation of awkwardness rushed over her, she remembered seeing the man who stood across from the shop.

"You know, Quinn, there is one other thing that was strange today." Nikki paused as they reached the door of the police station. She winced as she glanced at the other officers. "I'm sorry, Detective Grant."

"Please, call me Quinn." He smiled, though the expression faded, replaced by the intensity of his gaze. "Now, what else was strange?"

"I was on my way to take Coco home, and I noticed this man." Nikki sighed and shook her head. "It's probably nothing, and it's silly to even tell you about it, but something seemed so off."

"Who was he?" He pulled a notepad from his pocket. "It's not silly at all. When a crime like this is committed, it's important to pay attention to every detail. You never know where a clue might come from."

"I don't know who he is. But the way he was

staring at the shop, it made me think he was really invested in what happened there. Maybe he knew Bryan? I don't know for sure."

"Can you describe him to me?"

"He had short, brown hair and was quite tall with a bit of a belly. He looked to be in his fifties. I followed him a short time, and saw him go inside a real estate agency, the one on Main Street." She shrugged. "It's more than likely nothing, but I thought you should know."

"About what time?" He didn't look up from his notepad.

"It was about one-thirty." Nikki pushed the door to the police station open. "Like I said, it's probably nothing."

"It may be, or it may not be. It's not unheard of for criminals to return to the scene of their crime. Thanks again for your time, Nikki. If you think of anything else, you have my number." Quinn locked eyes with her as she stood in the threshold of the doorway.

"Yes, I do." Nikki stepped all the way through the door and let it fall closed behind her.

CHAPTER 4

As Nikki started off towards her apartment, a wave of tiredness washed over her. She had been through some ups and downs throughout the day, and now all she could think about was getting some rest. However, as she walked past Bryan's shop in the direction of her apartment, something else caught her attention. The shop was still roped off with wide, yellow police tape. However, it appeared to be empty. It was dark inside. Yet a second before, a flash of light had drawn her attention. As she watched, a flashlight beam traveled across the interior of the shop. It traced along rows of leashes and collars, sparkling as it struck metal surfaces. Her heart pounded as she wondered why anyone would be inside with a flashlight. The police had plenty of equipment to light up the shop, but she was sure that the electricity still worked. She could only guess that whoever was inside, was up to something. But what? Why would anyone risk prowling around a crime scene?

A quick glance up and down the street revealed that there was no traffic, and no sign of any police vehicles nearby. Could it be an officer doing some kind of extra search? But why with a flashlight? Her curiosity drove her right into the alley beside the store. She crept close to one of the windows on the side of the building. It was small, and high. She had to stand on her tiptoes to peer through it. As she did she saw a figure pacing through the shop. His flashlight swung past the small window. She winced, and drew back. Had he seen her?

As Nikki's heart pounded she considered whether she should run. But an instant later she was back on her toes, with her eyes locked to the man inside. This time she recognized him. It was the same man that she'd seen earlier at the café. The man who wore a motorcycle jacket. He certainly wasn't a police officer, and certainly didn't belong inside the shop. Determined to find out just what he was up to, she decided to call the police. They needed to know that their crime scene was being invaded, and she needed to know why. As she dug in her purse for her phone, a sinking sensation rippled through her. She didn't have her phone. She'd left it on Quinn's desk during their conversation. Which meant that she had no way of calling for help. She could run to the next shop, or even to one of the nearby houses, but that meant she would have to leave, which would give the man a chance to get away. What if he was gone by the time the police arrived?

At least if Nikki stayed, she might get an idea of what he was doing, something that she could share with the police when she was able to contact them. She got back up on her toes and looked through the window again. He seemed to be more determined than ever. As she watched, he pulled paintings from the walls. Then he began to shove shelving away from the walls. It became clear that he was looking for something, and had no intention of leaving until he found it. When he bent down to pry at the floorboards, she wondered what could be driving him to search so thoroughly.

Nikki climbed up on a loose brick in an attempt to get a better view. The brick tumbled loose of the foundation, and her body slammed forward against the wall with a loud thump. She cringed as pain burst through her body, but a moment later she realized she had more to be concerned about. Had he heard anything inside the shop? She peered through the window just in time to catch him looking in her direction. As they locked eyes her chest tightened. She knew in that instant that she had been spotted, and within seconds he could be outside, demanding to know what she saw. Uncertain of his purpose for being there, she was aware that he could be the person who killed Bryan. Would he kill her, too? She wasn't going to stick around to find out.

Nikki burst into a run. As she propelled herself through the familiar streets, and passed the shops and homes that she knew so well, she was sure that someone inside would help her. But she couldn't risk slowing down, or stopping. If she did, the man in the shop might be right on top of her. If only she hadn't peeked in the window, if only she hadn't been too curious to resist, she might not be in this situation. Her chest threatened to burst from the intense exertion as she ran as fast as she possibly could. The only place she could think to go was home. It was where she felt the safest. However, as she reached her apartment, she realized it might not have been the best decision. She would be alone, and her neighbors weren't the type to pay attention to anyone else's business. She fumbled with her keys. Once she managed to get the key into the lock, she shoved her way through the door and slammed it closed behind her. She leaned back against the door and closed her eyes for just a second. She listened for the sound of footsteps on the walkway. Had he followed her? All she heard was silence.

Only then did Nikki peer out through her windows to see if the man had followed her. Once she was satisfied that he wasn't lurking outside she began to double-check that all of her windows and the front door were locked. Again, she reached in her purse for her phone, only to recall that she didn't have it. She didn't want to go outside, yet. She perched on the edge of the couch and thought about what she had seen. She was sure it was the same man that she'd seen in the café that morning. She recalled the words the two men exchanged, and how unsettling they could be. They may have been having an innocent conversation, but it may have also been about Bryan. Why else would the man be searching through the shop when no one else was there? Maybe there was a reasonable explanation for what happened. Maybe she was overreacting.

Nikki took a few deep breaths. She was okay.

He hadn't followed her. He might not have even seen her. Maybe he'd just looked at the window, and she thought he met her eyes. Her thoughts were interrupted by the sound of a knock on the front door. Her body stiffened in reaction to it. Would a murderer knock on the front door? She wasn't sure.

After another set of knocks Nikki convinced herself to get up. She approached the door as quietly as she could. Maybe whoever was outside would assume she wasn't home and leave.

As she stood on the other side of the door, she held her breath. Seconds passed. She thought perhaps whoever it was had given up and walked away. Then a third set of knocks, firmer this time, shook the front door. Her stomach twisted as she realized that whoever it was outside, knew that she was inside, and they weren't giving up.

Slowly Nikki reached for the door knob. With one hand raised in the air, prepared to defend herself, she pulled the door open.

"Hey Nikki." Quinn smiled, though it faded when he noticed her balled up fist. "Is everything okay?"

"Sorry Quinn." She dropped her hand and blushed. "I didn't know it was you."

"Well, that's reassuring." He raised an eyebrow.

"But apparently you were expecting someone else that you wanted to knock out?" He held her phone out to her. "You left this at the station, I just wanted to return it."

"Oh, thank you." She grabbed her phone.

"Nikki." He looked into her eyes. "What's going on? What has you spooked?"

"It's probably nothing, I'm just being silly." She shook her head, but then took the time to look in all directions past him. "There was no one else around the apartment when you walked up, was there?"

"No, not that I noticed." He frowned. "Do you mind if I come inside?"

"Sure, of course." Nikki stepped aside to allow him in, and closed the door behind him. Then she locked it.

"You've got to tell me what's wrong." Quinn turned to face her. "Did something happen?"

Nikki stared into his eyes, then everything about what she witnessed at the shop and the café earlier in the day began to spill out.

"I thought he saw me, but now I'm not so sure, and I was going to call the police, but I didn't have my phone."

"Sh, it's all right." He wrapped his arms around her.

The sudden sensation of his closeness did nothing to calm her down. Instead it resulted in her being more nervous, and distracted at the same time. Still, she took a moment to appreciate what it felt like to be in his arms before she pulled away.

"I'm okay, really, I was just a little startled." She sighed. "Like I said, it's probably nothing."

"I'm sending someone over to check the shop out now." Quinn fired off a text, then tucked his phone back into his pocket. "Listen, do you really think he saw you?"

"I don't know." Nikki crossed her arms and gazed at him. "I can't be sure. But I'm pretty sure he didn't follow me. Which means he doesn't know where I live."

"Still, if there's any chance that you're in danger you need to be extra-cautious. Make sure you have your phone on you at all times, no leaving it behind." Quinn locked his eyes to hers.

"Yes, I'll be more careful." She tightened her grip on her phone.

"If anything seems off, anything at all, you don't hesitate to call me." He placed his hand on her shoulder and continued to gaze into her eyes. "Understand?"

"Yes. I would have called, if I'd had my phone

on me." Nikki nodded. His touch was comforting. "Thanks, Quinn. For being here, and for bringing my phone to me. I know how busy you must be."

"Never too busy to check on you." He let his hand fall back to his side. "Stay safe, okay?"

"I will." She nodded, then walked him to the door.

"Make sure you lock up as soon as I leave." He glanced back at her.

"Thanks, Quinn." She nodded again, then closed the door. When she didn't hear any footsteps, she realized he was waiting for her to lock the door. She turned both locks and heard him walk off down the sidewalk.

Nikki closed her eyes and rested her forehead on the door for a moment. She couldn't imagine what he must think of her. He'd arrived to find her ready to defend herself, and then had to lecture her about leaving her phone behind. It was nice to know that he was concerned about her, but she couldn't help wonder if he might view her as more of a burden than a benefit. She promised herself she would be more careful. Still, a shiver of fear crept up along her spine that wouldn't cease until she checked all of the windows and doors again. Satisfied that they were locked, she realized that the only way that she was going to relax was to find out what really happened to Bryan.

Nikki decided that the best place to start was finding out more about him. She settled on the couch with her computer and began to dig into his past. It didn't take long for her to find out that he was well-known in the dog community, and a very respected designer. She found his name mentioned in several articles and on various websites. In general, every comment about him was a glowing one. However, she noticed that Bryan himself hadn't made any recent posts. He'd gone from being a daily blogger, showing off his latest fashions, and drumming up support from his fan club, to zero posts for at least the past week.

Once Nikki hit this dead end, she began looking into the woman that Quinn had named. Heather Cantrells. She claimed that Bryan clipped her on her motorcycle. Quinn had mentioned that a witness heard the sound of a motorcycle around the time of Bryan's murder. It wasn't hard to find information about her as she was very active on social media. Soon, Nikki discovered that she worked at a small gas station, located just outside of Dahlia. She also found out that she was twenty-three, and appeared to be single. As she combed through some of her posts, she discovered that Heather had been posting quite a bit lately, and many of her posts had Bryan's name in them. She detailed how he clipped her motorcycle the night before, and then fled the scene. She threatened to have him arrested, and insisted that he needed to be prepared to hear from her lawyers. She even made a custom meme that featured Bryan's face in the center of a 'worst driver ever' award. Clearly, she was not happy about the accident. However, she did reply to her friends that she was unharmed, then went on to detail what could have happened to her if she hadn't been paying attention.

Heather had generated a lot of support for herself, while many people were quite angry with Bryan. Not as angry as Heather, though. Nikki wiped her eyes, and glanced at the clock. Several hours had slipped by. She made herself a snack, then returned to the computer. She searched for any connection between Heather and the man she'd seen in the motorcycle jacket. However, he did not seem to be one of her friends, or business contacts.

After hours of research on both Bryan and Heather, Nikki decided it would be worth it to pay Heather a visit. Maybe she would be willing to share something with her, as she wasn't with the police. Plus, she wanted to see face-to-face, just how angry Heather was. Angry enough to kill?

As Nikki glanced towards the window she realized that the sun had begun to rise. She'd been at it all night, and though she should be exhausted, she felt energized instead. After a hearty breakfast, she took a long shower to wash away her fear from the day before. She wanted to focus on solving the murder, not why she should be afraid. With Quinn as a friend, what reason did she have to be afraid? She knew that he was just a phone call away. The day before she'd been worried that someone might be lurking outside of her apartment, but now she felt more confident. Yesterday was probably just a little paranoia.

Nikki pulled her light brown hair back into a ponytail, took a deep breath, and focused her energy on the matter at hand. She would help find out what happened to Bryan, then everything could get back to normal. As she headed out the door she greeted the early morning sun with a smile. When she turned to close her door and lock it, she was confronted by the sight of a note taped to her door. At first, she thought it might just be something that Quinn left behind. However, as she read the thick, black letters on the paper, her heart began to race.

I know where you live.

Nikki's eyes widened as she read it over again. Could it be a joke? Or was it left by the man in the motorcycle jacket? She quickly glanced around to see if anyone remained nearby. She recognized a few of her neighbors heading out to work, but none that would put such a note on her door. Someone wanted her to see this message, and she knew exactly what it meant. She needed to be careful, or she was going to be next.

CHAPTER 5

Nikki took a deep breath and tried to decide what to do next. Her instincts told her to rip down the note and tear it to pieces. She didn't want to be frightened by it. But logic warned her not to touch it, and to call Quinn. He'd made her promise that she would be more careful and call him if anything came up. Although she hoped that this might just be a prank of some kind, she couldn't take the chance of being wrong. She dialed Quinn's number and waited for him to pick up. Only after the phone rang several times did she remember just how early it was. He likely was still asleep, or just on the road to work for the day. She didn't want to bother him first thing in the morning.

She was about to hang up, when she heard his voice on the line.

"Nikki, you're up early."

"I didn't sleep, actually." Nikki winced as she knew that probably wasn't the best thing to share.

"I'm sorry to hear that. Were you too worried? I would have sent a patrol officer to watch your apartment, if you were."

"No, I just got caught up in some research." She cleared her throat. "Quinn, this is probably just a joke, but as I went to leave my apartment this morning I found a note taped to my door. I haven't touched it, I thought I should call you first."

"A note?" His tone sharpened with interest. "What does it say?"

"It says, I know where you live." Nikki frowned. "That's it, nothing more. It's not exactly a threat."

"It's an implied threat. You were right not to touch it. Stay right where you are, I'll be there in five minutes."

"Are you sure, Quinn? It's probably nothing." Nikki gazed at the note and shuddered at the thought of a murderer standing outside and carefully taping it to her door. How had she not heard anything? Why didn't she sense something?

"I'll be right there." He hung up the phone.

Nikki sighed as she began to pace back and forth. By the time Quinn arrived, she was covered in a thin layer of sweat.

"Hey." He jogged up to her from the parking lot. "Are you okay?"

"Yes, I'm fine. It's just a note. The worst thing it could give me is a paper cut." She flashed him a smile.

"Nikki, this is serious." He gazed at the note, then looked over at her. "I'm going to bag it for evidence, and we'll check it for prints. I want to know who left this here."

"It could have just been a prank. There are quite a few teenagers that live around here." Nikki shrugged and shoved her hands into her pockets. "I don't want to make a big deal out of it."

"But it is a big deal." Quinn retrieved some gloves from his pocket, then pulled them on. "What are the chances that someone played a prank on the same night that you caught someone breaking into a crime scene?"

"Maybe someone saw me running home, looking frightened." Nikki bit into her bottom lip. "I'm not scared, Quinn."

"Why not?" He bagged the note, then turned to

face her. "Whoever did this was right outside your apartment door."

"And all he did was leave a note." She forced a smile to her lips and shrugged. "See? If he was really some kind of criminal, if he even was a he, then why stop at leaving a note? Why didn't he try to hurt me?"

"I'm not sure, but I'm grateful that he didn't."

"So am I, and I'm going to take it as a good sign. Maybe there really is nothing to be concerned about. I presume you didn't catch the man that was in Bryan's shop?" Nikki looked at him as hope welled up within her.

"I'm afraid not. The cameras have been disabled, and there's no sign of a break-in. We're really not sure how he got in. But we are still looking for him." He met her eyes. "Why don't you let me put a patrol car at your apartment tonight?"

"Quinn, there's no need for that. I'm fine. I promise. I called you, didn't I?" Nikki raised an eyebrow.

"Yes, you did." He smiled for the first time. "Please, make sure that you continue to do so."

"I will." Nikki thought about sharing her intentions to visit Heather, but she decided against it. He wanted her safe and as far from the investigation as she could be. Seeking out a suspect, didn't exactly check those boxes. "Thanks, Quinn."

"I'll catch up with you later." He studied her a moment longer, then headed back to his car. She watched him go, then walked towards her own car. As she opened the car door, she checked the back-seat. Yes, she was paranoid, and the only way out of it was by the case being solved. If she could speed up the process she would.

As Nikki drove towards the gas station where Heather worked, she felt confident that Heather would be there. From her posts it appeared that she worked the morning shift. She parked in the nearly empty parking lot, then headed inside. She spotted Heather right away, behind the counter, with a cup of coffee in one hand, and a magazine in the other.

"Good morning." Nikki did her best to sound cheerful.

"Morning." Heather lowered the magazine some. "Would you like some coffee?"

"No thanks, I'm just here to talk to you, actually." Nikki paused in front of the counter.

"Me?" Heather narrowed her eyes. Then they widened with recognition. "I remember you. You were in Bryan's shop yesterday."

"Yes, I was."

"You're the reason that the cops knew why I was there." Heather sighed. "I guess that you relayed the way I talked to him."

"There was a surveillance camera."

"Yes, there are cameras here, too, but they don't catch audio. So, it was you that told the police what I said, right?" Heather gazed at her from behind thick lashes, made thicker with layers of mascara.

"Yes, I did." Nikki cleared her throat. "But only what you said, nothing more."

"Thanks for that, I guess." Heather pursed her lips, then blew a breath through her nose. "If you knew what he did to me, you wouldn't blame me for saying those things."

"What did he do to you?" Nikki studied her.

"He was driving like a maniac. He was going much faster than the speed limit and kept weaving all over the road. I saw him coming, so I tried to stay to the side, but it was impossible to avoid him. If I hadn't been paying attention, he would have killed me."

"I'm so sorry, that must have been so frightening." Nikki frowned as she leaned against the counter.

"It was. I thought I was going to die. But I managed to save myself. Then he didn't even bother to stop, to apologize, to admit that he was wrong. I thought maybe he would continue on and kill someone else. That's why I called the police to make a report." Heather sighed and lowered her eyes. "I didn't expect any of this to happen. Of course, I wouldn't have made all of those threats if I had known."

"You had good reason to be upset and angry." Nikki straightened up and began to look around the store. "He could have killed you."

"Yes, I was, and I still am. But that doesn't make me a killer. So, next time you talk to the cops, why don't you try telling them that?" Heather set her cup of coffee down on the counter.

"I didn't mean to upset you." Nikki turned back to face her.

"You just wanted to know if I'm a murderer?" Heather rolled her eyes, then turned to the register. "I have things to do."

"I understand." Nikki started to say more, but decided against it. Heather had made up her mind about her, and nothing she said was going to change that. At least, not at the moment.

As Nikki left the shop she wondered if Heather might be capable of murder. She certainly seemed angry, but she was right, being angry didn't make her a killer.

~

Nikki drove back towards Dahlia with thoughts of Heather and Bryan on her mind. How would she feel if it had been her that Bryan almost killed? Would she want some kind of revenge? She doubted it, she wasn't a vengeful person by nature. But she'd also never been in that situation. As she entered Dahlia she tried to push the thoughts from her mind. It was almost time for Princess' walk, and she wanted to be able to greet Mrs. Whitter with a positive attitude. She knew that the woman was likely quite stressed, and she didn't want to add to that stress.

When she drove down the long driveway to the vast house, she took some time to appreciate all that Mrs. Whitter did for her dog. She loved Princess like her own child, and as silly as it might seem for her to be so concerned over a birthday party, she knew that it meant a lot more to Mrs. Whitter than just that.

With a light knock on the door she alerted Mrs. Whitter to her presence. It was Princess who responded however, with excited yips at the door, and a bit of scratching from the other side.

"Hi Princess." Nikki clucked her tongue and smiled. A moment later, Mrs. Whitter opened the door.

"Oh. Nikki, thank goodness you're here, and a little early, too. I'm so glad. I am just beside myself." Mrs. Whitter pressed her hands against her cheeks. "Just one day left and I still haven't found a gift for Princess."

"Don't worry, Mrs. Whitter, I know you'll find something absolutely perfect." Nikki smiled at her and set aside her concerns about Heather.

"Thank you, I needed to hear that. I'm going to spend the day shopping, so if I'm not here when you're done with your walk, please just make sure Princess has everything she needs. And text me once you drop her off, okay?" Mrs. Whitter met her eyes, her own tight and anxious.

"Yes, of course. I'll spend some extra time with her, too." Nikki scooped up Princess and smiled as the dog licked her cheek. "We can hang out a bit, can't we, Princess?"

The dog gave a light yip and wiggled in her arms.

"I think that's a yes." Mrs. Whitter laughed, then

gave Nikki a pat on the shoulder. "I don't know what we would do without you, Nikki." She hurried off to retrieve her purse. "I just hope I can find something."

"I'm sure you will. Good luck!" Nikki waved to Mrs. Whitter as she left the house with Princess at her side.

Nikki walked Princess through the park first, but was drawn towards Bryan's shop. She hoped that being near it again might help her to remember something from the day before that would give her more clarity on what the man was doing inside the shop. As she neared it she noticed a man who had crossed the yellow tape. He paused beside each window and peered inside. Her heart skipped a beat as she wondered for a second if it might be the same man that she'd seen inside the shop the day before. Had he left the note? As the man turned, she realized that he was much taller, and thicker around the middle, than the man she'd seen inside the shop. Instead, she realized, he was the man she had followed the day before. The one who had disappeared inside the real estate agency.

Nikki walked towards him as curiosity overwhelmed her. This was the second time she'd caught him so interested in the shop. But why? Maybe she could get his name this time.

"Excuse me, are you supposed to be past that tape?" Nikki paused just outside of it.

"It's all right, I'm not hurting anything." He glanced back at her. "The officer that was here said they've done the search inside, and will be taking down the tape later today."

"Oh." She cleared her throat. "If you don't mind me asking, why are you so interested in the shop?"

"Ah, you must be a local." He arched an eyebrow. "Nosy."

"I am a local." Nikki smiled and lowered her eyes. "I'm not nosy, just curious. You seem so interested in what's inside."

"I plan to rent it, that's why. I want to be sure nothing has changed too much." He looked through the front window.

"The owner of the shop was killed here, doesn't that bother you?" Nikki looked into his eyes.

"Why should it?" He gazed at her. "It's not as if I believe in ghosts. Do you?"

"I'm not sure, but I do know I wouldn't be so quick to rent a place where someone had been murdered. What if the killer comes back?" Nikki held tightly to Princess' leash as she tried to find out what he knew about the murder.

"Why would he? Bryan is dead, there's no reason for the murderer to come back." He peered through one of the windows. "I just hope they do a good job of cleaning it up."

"You knew Bryan?" Nikki swallowed back a rush of disgust in reaction to his flippant attitude.

"Sure, I knew him, he stole this place right out from under me." He glanced back at her. "Some good guy, right? Business is business. The place will be for rent, and I plan to rent it." He crossed his arms. "Nothing is going to stop me this time."

Nikki was startled by just how cold he was. She recalled Gina telling her about an argument between Bryan and another man, over the shop. She guessed this must be him.

"What kind of business will you have here?" She shifted her tone to one of interest.

"An electronics shop. Everything from computers to alarms." He pulled out his wallet, then picked out a business card. As he handed it over, he smiled. "It will be a great resource for the people of this town. Far better than dog fashion." He sneered. "Do you really think dogs care about the color of their clothes?"

"I don't think it matters as long as the dogs are comfortable. The owners enjoy what their dogs wear, and the outfits often serve a purpose. Like to keep off the sun or to keep them warm." Nikki shrugged.

"Sure, okay." He rolled his eyes and turned back to the building. "Trust me, once my shop opens people around here won't even remember Bryan."

"I'm sure that's not true." She felt her heartbeat quicken as anger rocketed through her. "Bryan was a very good man, and many people in this town became friends with him, even during the short time that he was here."

"Well, then those people are terrible judges of character." He turned towards her, his brows knitted, and his eyes hard. "Because Bryan was a criminal, who associated with criminals, and this town is far better off without him. The only reason he was able to rent this place out from under me, is because someone strong-armed the real estate agent. Just to be clear, what I mean is, someone threatened her, until she complied." He stared at Nikki, his eyes still fierce. "Don't expect me to shed a tear over a man that is willing to do business that way."

"Who threatened her?" She stared right back at him, unfazed by his attempt at intimidation.

"That's not my business." He shrugged, then walked along the building.

Nikki considered going after him, to question him further, but from his demeanor she could tell that he didn't plan on saying another word to her. Plus, she didn't want to risk him turning his temper on her. She couldn't shake the thought of Bryan being a criminal, and being involved with criminals. Was that just a way to deflect her attention from what he was up to? She glanced down at the card in her hand.

Electronics and More. Royce Blake.

That was definitely the man Gina had mentioned being in the café having an argument with Bryan.

Nikki continued towards Mrs. Whitter's house. Princess lunged forward as they neared her house. She began to bark and pull at the leash.

"Oh, aren't you excited to get home?" Nikki smiled. "Maybe Mrs. Whitter is right about you, maybe you do suspect that something is going on. Are you getting excited?"

Princess hopped back and forth a bit, then lunged towards the house again. Nikki laughed at her enthusiasm. As they got closer Nikki heard an alarm. The closer she got the louder it rang. Her heart skipped a beat as she got closer to the house and she realized it was Mrs. Whitter's alarm. Her heartbeat raced as she pulled out her keys to unlock the door. Maybe it was a false alarm. Maybe Mrs. Whitter had accidently set it off. Perhaps Mrs. Whitter had come home early, which meant she might have had good luck on her shopping trip. But why hadn't she turned off the alarm, yet?

Before Nikki could slide the key into the lock, the door swung open on its own.

"Mrs. Whitter, are you home?" Nikki peeked her head through the door.

As she stepped further inside, her heart raced as she didn't hear a response from Mrs. Whitter. Was there someone else in the house?

CHAPTER 6

Danger made Nikki gasp just before she noticed the broken glass from the window next to the front door. She quickly picked up Princess and held her tightly. She knew she should call the police, but first she needed to make sure Mrs. Whitter wasn't in the house, that she wasn't in danger.

"Mrs. Whitter? Mrs. Whitter, are you here?" Her heart pounded as she wondered whether Mrs. Whitter might be hurt. Nikki rushed through the house, but didn't see any sign of who might have been in the house. She checked every room, but found no one.

After she entered her code into the alarm panel to turn it off, she pulled out her phone and dialed

Mrs. Whitter's cell phone. When she answered, a rush of relief threatened to knock her off her feet.

"Where are you, Mrs. Whitter?"

"I'm shopping, like I told you. Is everything all right, Nikki? You sound upset."

"The alarm was going off, and the door was open when we got back from our walk. The window by the door was smashed. I just needed to make sure you were safe. I'm going to call the police."

"The police? Oh dear, oh no." She gasped. "Are you safe?"

"I think so. It's okay, Mrs. Whitter, whoever it was must have left when they heard the alarm."

"I'll be there as soon as I can." Mrs. Whitter hung up the phone.

As soon as she did, Nikki called Quinn. She held her breath as he answered.

"Nikki, I haven't gotten any hits on the note yet, but the crime lab is still analyzing some—"

"Quinn, someone broke into Mrs. Whitter's house. When I got here, the alarm was going off and the glass was broken, no one was inside." She looked at the broken glass.

"I'll be right there, stay on the phone with me." The urgency in his voice frightened her.

"It's okay, Quinn, I'm safe."

"There could still be someone in the house. I'm on my way, just stay on the phone with me. I'm only a few minutes away." She could hear traffic in the background. "Tell me what you saw when you got there."

"The alarm was going off. I went to unlock the door, and the door was already unlocked, and open. I thought maybe Mrs. Whitter had come home early, but she hadn't. I've already spoken with her. She was still out shopping, but she's on her way home now." Nikki paced through the house.

"Good, I'll need to speak with her. What happened when you went inside? I'll be there in two minutes."

"I noticed the broken window. I looked through the house, but there was no sign of anyone." Nikki held Princess close. "I have no idea who it was."

"I'm here, I'll be right in." He hung up the phone.

Nikki kept her phone clenched in her hand as she carried Princess back to the front door. She watched as Quinn jogged up to the door. She felt so relieved to see him.

"Nikki." Quinn continued to hold her gaze as he put his hands on her shoulders. "I'm going to take a look around, okay?" They turned to the sound of a security patrol car pulling into the driveway. "They're a bit late." He sighed. "Give me a minute." He walked over to the security guard as he got out of the car. Quinn said something to him, his face was stern, but she couldn't hear what he said. The security guard's shoulders slumped, then he got in the car and drove off. Quinn walked back to Nikki. "There are patrol cars behind me. You and Princess stay out here in my car, until they get here. Okay?"

"It's okay, I'm okay." Nikki forced a smile to her lips despite the chaos.

"Good." He smiled, then headed towards the house.

Before she could even get the door to Quinn's car open, Mrs. Whitter pulled into the driveway. Her compact car skidded to a stop, and she leaped out the moment she turned the engine off.

"Oh Princess, my poor baby, you must be so scared." She ran straight over to Nikki and gently took the dog out of her arms.

"She's okay, Mrs. Whitter, you should have seen how brave she was. I think she knew that something was wrong before I did. She kept barking and tugging at the leash. I thought she was just excited to get home, but now I think she knew someone had been inside." Nikki rubbed her hands along her arms and glanced towards the house. "Quinn is inside taking a look around."

"Oh yes, wonderful, so good of him." Mrs. Whitter winced as another police car pulled into the driveway. "Must those sirens be so loud?" She covered Princess' ears.

"Mrs. Whitter, I'm sorry. I didn't see who was in the house." Nikki frowned as she studied her. "I must have been too late."

"My dear girl, you have nothing to apologize for." Mrs. Whitter grasped one of her hands and gave it a squeeze. "I'm just so glad that you weren't hurt. I know I can always trust you to protect my Princess."

"I always will." Nikki nodded as she smiled.

"Mrs. Whitter." Quinn walked towards them from inside the house. "Could I speak to you for a moment?"

"Certainly." She stroked the dog's fur.

"Did you find anything?" Nikki met his eyes.

He stared at her for a second, then directed his attention to Mrs. Whitter again.

"Who was the last person to leave the house?" Quinn pulled out his tablet.

"I was." She nodded. "I left just a few minutes after Nikki left for her walk with Princess."

"And were you in any kind of rush? Distracted?" Quinn looked up from his tablet and into her eyes.

"I was in a bit of a rush yes, maybe a little distracted. What are you getting at?" She straightened her shoulders.

"The kitchen door was unlocked, but closed. I just wondered if perhaps you might have forgotten to lock it." Quinn tapped the screen. "It happens to all of us."

"Not to me it doesn't," Mrs. Whitter snapped. "You think just because I'm an old lady I don't value my home or my possessions?" She shook her head. "Well, you're wrong. I value them both. I am not foolish. I do value my things, you know?"

"I meant no offense." Quinn held up one hand. "These are questions I have to ask to help us figure out who it was that broke into your home and what they were after. I think they might have exited through the kitchen door."

"Sorry, some offense taken." She held Princess out to Nikki. "Perhaps it's time I took a look inside myself. I'd like to know if this horrible criminal left anything behind."

"I can take you on a walk-through to check for missing valuables, but you must be careful not to touch anything. The house will be searched, and dusted for prints."

"Oh no, it absolutely will not!" She placed her hands on her hips as she raised her voice.

"Ma'am, we must conduct an investigation." Quinn narrowed his eyes, then glanced over at Nikki.

"Mrs. Whitter, it's important to find out who broke into your home, isn't it?" Nikki stroked Princess' fur to calm her.

"Yes, of course, but it's far more important for my home to be in tip-top shape for the party tomorrow. I can't have people pawing through my things, and fingerprint dust everywhere. I can't, and I won't." She stomped one foot against the driveway. "I won't have it!"

"Why don't we just start with the walk-through, then we can go from there?" Quinn flashed her a warm and reassuring smile.

Nikki was impressed with how well he remained calm. Mrs. Whitter could be quite stubborn, and when she decided she wanted things a certain way, that was the way they would be, no matter what it took. As she watched Quinn lead the way into the house, she decided she was better off remaining outside. She looked into Princess' eyes and smiled.

"Don't worry, Princess, everything is going to be just fine."

The dog licked her cheek. Nikki wondered who was reassuring who.

When Quinn and Mrs. Whitter came back outside, Nikki noticed that Mrs. Whitter appeared a bit calmer.

"I know that you have a very important job to do, but this isn't important."

"It is important." Quinn turned to face her. "Someone invaded your home."

"Maybe. But whoever it was didn't take anything, it really doesn't seem like that big of a deal."

"It's still a big deal." Nikki walked up to them both. "Mrs. Whitter, you really should let them find out what they can about who broke in."

"Now Nikki, you know I love you." Mrs. Whitter narrowed her eyes. "But nothing is going to interfere with this party. I've been planning it for so long. You know how important it is to me."

"I do know." Nikki frowned. "But what if whoever broke in comes back?"

"I refuse to allow that." Mrs. Whitter held up her hands and shook her head firmly. "No one is going to make me feel unsafe in my home. The only reason someone was able to get in was because no one was here. I will upgrade my security, and I'm sure that Detective Quinn here will authorize added patrol for this neighborhood, especially during the party." She glanced at Quinn. "Isn't that right, Detective?"

"I'm sure that we can arrange that." Quinn slid his hands into his pockets. "I certainly can't force you to allow us to dust for prints, it's your choice. But I must warn you, there is a good chance that the person who was in your house was looking for something in particular. I can only assume that is why they didn't take anything. Now, either they took something that you're not aware of, or they were startled by the alarm going off or Nikki coming back, which means that they might actually return."

"I'm not stupid, Detective, I know the reasons that someone might have broken in. I also know that there is very little chance that the person will return after the alarm went off and they were almost caught. I will get the window fixed, today." Mrs. Whitter clapped her hands together. "No, the party must go on, and I won't have my guests frightened off by any of this." She held her arms out for Princess. "Now, Nikki I know you have things to do."

"I do have other dogs to walk." She handed Princess over to Mrs. Whitter.

"Before you take off, I'd like to talk to you." Quinn caught Nikki's eye, then turned his attention back to Mrs. Whitter. "If anything changes, if you feel uncomfortable about anything at all, please do not hesitate to contact us."

"Thanks, sweetheart." Mrs. Whitter held up Princess so that she could lick his cheek. "Isn't he sweet, Princess? Don't worry, we'll be just fine." She waved to them both, then stepped back inside the house.

Quinn opened his mouth as if he might say something more, but Mrs. Whitter firmly shut the door.

"She's impossible." He shook his head as he turned back to Nikki.

"Oh, that's nothing." Nikki smiled. "She was being nice to you."

"Nice? You should have heard her put me in my place while we were inside." He shoved his hands in his pockets. "There's nothing I can do, though, my hands are tied on all of this."

"It's okay, Quinn. I know that you did what you could. Maybe Mrs. Whitter is right, and there's nothing to be concerned about." Nikki crossed her arms then took a deep breath. "All of this seems so much worse because of what happened to Bryan. We're on high alert."

"As you should be." He met her eyes. "It's very important to take the proper precautions right now. Especially after the note you found on your door this morning."

"I'm sure it's nothing." She waved her hand and started to walk down the driveway.

"Excuse me." Quinn caught her arm gently by the elbow. "It is not nothing. Why aren't you taking this seriously?"

"I am taking it seriously. I just don't want to get too paranoid." Nikki sighed as she looked back at the house. "Look at Mrs. Whitter, someone broke into her house, and she's not willing to be the slightest bit afraid, and me? Yesterday I thought that someone saw me through a window, and I was scared. That's silly. I hope that you are able to get this solved, of course, but I don't really need to be worried. The note was probably just a prank."

"That's what has me concerned. I'm not asking you to be scared, Nikki, but I do hope that you can take this seriously."

"I am." She met his eyes briefly, then looked down at her shoes. "I'll be cautious. But I do have to get going. I have dogs waiting for me."

"That does sound important." Quinn nodded. "But maybe I should have an officer go with you."

"Quinn." She crossed her arms as she studied him. "I get it. I understand that you are concerned about me, and I even appreciate it. But I can handle things on my own."

"Just be careful, please?" His voice softened as he took a step closer to her. She saw him transition from a detective, to a friend, and felt herself relax.

"I will be. Thank you, Quinn."

As Nikki walked off down the driveway, she suspected that he continued to watch her. She was tempted to look back over her shoulder to confirm that, but she resisted. Already, she had a hard time maintaining her cool around him, she didn't need to make it even clearer that she still fought a puppy dog crush on him.

As Nikki collected each dog she did her best to focus only on the animal, and give each one the time and attention that she always did. Still, she found herself walking a bit more briskly than usual. As she strolled through the park, the familiar surroundings allowed her to relax. She drank in the sight of the green leaves that fluttered in the sunlight, and the wide-open, blue sky.

By the time Nikki began to return the dogs to their houses, she felt more secure and had convinced herself that she was right. She'd let herself get too worked up over the sight of the man in Bryan's shop, and then the note that was left on her door. The truth was, most people were good people, and there wasn't anyone out to get her. With only Coco left to take home, she slowed her pace and enjoyed a few extra minutes with him. When a squirrel bolted across the street, he lunged after it.

"Slow down!" Nikki tightened her grasp on the leash, and took a few steps back. When she collided with someone behind her, she gasped and spun around. "I'm so sorry." She lifted her eyes to the man's face, and another gasp silenced her.

"I'm sorry, I didn't mean to scare you."

"I know who you are." Nikki stumbled back and almost tripped on Coco's leash. Her heart slammed against her chest. The man that stood before her was the very same man that she'd seen in Bryan's shop. The one that saw her spying on him. She turned, and started to run.

"Wait! Please!" He began to run after her.

As Nikki tried to run even faster, her lungs began to burn. Coco panted at her side, but easily kept pace with her. Within moments the man caught up to her, and grabbed her by the shoulder.

CHAPTER 7

"Let go of me!" Nikki jerked free of his hand, and opened her mouth to scream.

"Just wait! I only want to talk to you." He stared hard into her eyes. "Please! I'm not going to hurt you."

"Talk to me?" Nikki stared back at him. "I know that you left that note on my door."

"What note?" He shook his head slowly. "I don't know anything about that." He pushed his blond hair back from his eyes, then took a slow breath. "Look, I know you have no reason to trust me, or to help me. I understand that."

"I certainly don't." Nikki shifted from one foot to the other. Although she knew that she should be afraid, she sensed something within him, something desperate, but not exactly violent. Coco growled at him, picking up on Nikki's fear. She patted his head to reassure him. "I saw you in Bryan's store. I know you broke in there to rob a dead man."

"A dead man?" He coughed, then glanced away. His jaw rippled as he looked back at her. "That dead man is my brother."

"Your brother?" Her eyes widened. "You're Bryan's brother?"

"The one and only." He shoved his hands into his pockets as his brown eyes raked over hers. "I had a right to be in the shop. I know that you saw me, and I know what you must have thought, but I wasn't trying to steal anything. I was just looking." He pulled his wallet from his pocket and flipped it open to reveal his driver's license. "See? Same last name."

"That doesn't prove anything." She gazed at the ID, then looked back up at him. "Tim Sashen. You sure weren't acting like you had a right to be there. The shop was still under police investigation." She looked into his brown eyes. Bryan had brown eyes, but she couldn't see any other similarities that indicated they were brothers.

"Maybe not a legal right." He winced, then shook his head. "I just had to be there. I had to try to figure out what happened to my brother. Wouldn't you do the same?"

"Most likely." Nikki frowned. "But you'd be better off just going to the police. I'm sure they would like to hear from you and to have your help to find your brother's killer."

"Maybe." He tilted his head to the side as he looked at her. "Or maybe they would just assume the same thing that you did. That I'm up to no good, that I should be feared."

"I'm not afraid of you." Nikki pursed her lips.

"A few minutes ago you were ready to scream at the top of your lungs. But you're not afraid?" He leaned a little closer to her. "I don't think I'm the one being dishonest."

"I didn't know who you were." Nikki stared at him. "When someone is killed, it causes everyone to be more on edge. Not only that, but someone had their home broken into today. I suppose you don't know anything about that either?"

"Why would I?" His eyes widened some and his lips curved into a mild smile.

"I am sorry for your loss." Nikki's tone remained even as she continued to study him. "I can only imagine how upset you must be. I'm sorry for assuming the worst about you."

"I'm the one that's sorry." He lowered his eyes for a moment, then looked back up at her. "For frightening you. But you don't have to be afraid of me. I just wanted the chance to tell you that. I saw how scared you were, and I didn't want you to continue to think that I might be looking for you."

"And yet, here we are." Nikki managed a smile, even as Coco gave a light growl.

"Yes, we are." His own smile spread wider. "I have a lot to deal with while I'm here. I'm sure we'll cross paths again." He offered her his hand. "It was nice to meet you."

"Nikki." She took his hand in a quick shake. She was still hesitant to give him any detailed information about herself. He claimed to be Bryan's brother, but she couldn't be completely sure of that, and he had still broken into the shop. "I admired your brother, he was very talented."

"Thanks. I wish we'd had the chance to be closer." He frowned, then looked towards Coco, who still growled. "I don't want to keep you. Thanks for listening."

"Sure." She nodded, then waited for him to walk away. He might seem genuine enough, but she still didn't want to turn her back on him.

Once he'd turned the corner, she urged Coco

along. As she walked, she tried to decide whether she believed Tim or not. He didn't seem to want to hurt her, but she also knew that she couldn't necessarily trust what he said. There was one person who could find out whether Tim told her the truth about being Bryan's brother. After she dropped off Coco, she placed a call to Quinn. After a few rings he picked up.

"Nikki, are you safe?"

"Are you going to ask me that every time I call?" She couldn't resist a smile.

"I don't know, will it make you call more, or less?" He laughed.

"I'm not sure." Nikki tipped her head back and forth. "I'll have to get back to you on that."

"Sure. It sounds like you are just fine. What's up?"

"Do you have some free time? There's something I'd like to discuss with you." Nikki continued on towards her apartment to get her car.

"Yes, I have some time. I'm just going over some evidence. Will you be here soon?"

"I'm just getting my car now, and I'll head straight over." Nikki hung up as she reached her driveway.

On the way to the police station Nikki's mind

swirled, she couldn't figure out Tim's intentions. She headed into the police station, hoping that Quinn would be able to help her sort it all out. She found him at a desk, focused on a monitor in front of him.

"Hi Quinn."

He looked away from the screen and smiled as she settled in the chair beside him.

"I'll just be a second. There's something that caught my eye in this video. I'm trying to verify it." Quinn looked back at the screen and pressed a key on the keyboard. The still image came to life. As she watched, she could see a car driving erratically, as well as a motorcycle two lanes over. She realized it must be surveillance video of the night Bryan clipped Heather's motorcycle. What she assumed to be Bryan's car veered to the right, towards the motorcycle, but the vehicles moved out of range of the camera before the actual collision. Quinn paused the video as another car came into view.

"There it is," he mumbled to himself as he made a note on his tablet.

"There what is?" Nikki leaned forward as she attempted to spot what had drawn his attention.

"I noticed that Bryan's car wasn't so much driving erratically, as evasively." Quinn tapped the screen. "This car is always behind his, and seems to be gaining on Bryan's car."

"You think he was being chased?" Her eyes widened at the thought.

"I think it's possible. I've been checking every resource we have to see if I can get a clear view of the license plate on this car, or the driver, unfortunately it's all too blurry. I'm hoping the crime lab can clean it up, but I doubt it." He sighed as he tossed his pen down beside his tablet.

"But if Bryan was being chased, why didn't he just say that?" Nikki frowned as she continued to stare at the screen. "Why didn't he call the police?"

"Very good questions." Quinn turned in his chair to face her. "Unfortunately, they are not easily answered."

"I spoke to a man named Royce Blake earlier this morning, when I took Princess for her walk. Apparently, he's the one who was in competition with Bryan to get the lease on that shop. He insisted that Bryan was involved with some pretty shady people." She frowned as she looked over at him. "I just dismissed it as nonsense, but maybe he was in some kind of trouble."

"Maybe. I'll have to speak with Royce about it."

Quinn made another note. Then looked up at her. "Now, what did you want to discuss?"

"I ran into someone else just now. The man who I saw sneaking around Bryan's shop." Nikki locked her eyes to his. "He claims to be Bryan's brother."

"Wait a minute." Quinn stared back into her eyes. "Are you saying you were just with the man who threatened you? Who broke into a crime scene? And you didn't think to call me?"

"Quinn." She narrowed her eyes some as she sensed anger in his tone. "We don't know if he left the note. He didn't hurt me. He apologized for scaring me. He said he had a right to be in the shop, because he was trying to find out what happened to his brother, and find anything that he might have left behind."

"Nikki." He ran his hand across his face, leaned back in his chair, and let out a long, slow breath. "Are you kidding me?"

"I can't call you every single time—"

"No, just the one time that you're with a criminal who threatened you." Quinn lowered his hand and gazed at her. "Is that so much to ask?"

"Quinn, you're not listening to me." Nikki gritted her teeth, then sighed. "I didn't even know that Bryan had a brother. Besides, he said he didn't leave that note on my door. I told you it was probably just a prank. He was kind to me, and said he saw how scared I was yesterday, and just wanted to make sure that I knew I had no reason to be afraid. How is that a bad thing?"

"And you believe him?" Quinn's eyes widened a little as his expression shifted from frustration, to wonder. "Why?"

"That's why I'm here." Nikki frowned. "I thought if anyone would know if Bryan had a brother, if this man was telling the truth, it would be you."

"I do know." Quinn nodded and grabbed his tablet. "Bryan has one brother. His name is Tim Sashen." He hit a few keys on the keyboard and pulled up a picture. "Is this the man you spoke to?"

"Yes, that's him." Her heart skipped a beat. "I guess he was telling the truth."

"He might have been telling the truth about who he was, but you still had reason to be frightened. He has quite a criminal history, everything from break-ins to assault." Quinn shook his head. "It's not a good idea to be alone with him. Most of his offenses are from a few years ago, but in my experience many criminals don't stop committing crimes, they just might go some time without getting caught."

"No matter his past, Bryan really is his brother, which means that he is grieving." Nikki sighed and folded her arms across her stomach as she gazed at the image on the screen. "He needs our help."

"You have such a good heart, Nikki." Quinn cleared his throat. "But we don't know that he's grieving."

Nikki sought his eyes, but he kept them fixated on the screen.

"What do you mean?"

"I mean, you told me that you saw Tim at the café, before Bryan was killed. Which means Tim didn't just show up in town to grieve his brother, he was already here." Quinn added a note to his tablet.

"You think he's a suspect? That he killed his own brother?" Nikki shivered at the idea.

"It's not pleasant to consider, but yes." Quinn glanced over at her. "He would have to be pretty ruthless to do it, which is why you need to tell me if he ever approaches you again. He may have just been trying to protect himself, since he knew that you had seen him in the shop. I'm going to do my best to pick him up and have a conversation with him. But if you see him again, you need to let me know." He paused then rubbed his hand along the curve of his cheek. "I should say, I would like it if you would contact me, right away."

"I will, Quinn." She smiled some at his effort to be less demanding. She sensed that he was still trying to find his footing as a detective. "Thanks for your help."

"Thank you for yours." He tapped his tablet. "You gave me a lot to work with."

"Good luck finding that car." Nikki stood up and gave him an awkward pat on his shoulder. He held her gaze as her hand lingered.

"Thanks."

Nikki wanted to say more. Instead, she drew her hand away, and headed out of the police station.

Once inside her car Nikki took a few minutes to think about what her next step might be. Quinn was right, Tim could easily be a suspect in his own brother's murder. She didn't want to think it, but she had no reason to eliminate him as a possibility. Then of course there was Heather, who might have been so angry from the accident that she decided to teach Bryan a lesson. Maybe things got out of hand, maybe she just wanted to threaten him not kill him. She rested her head back against the seat and closed her eyes. She also couldn't ignore the cold way that Royce spoke about Bryan. Could losing out on a lease really drive someone to kill? She considered it for a few moments, then recalled his insistence that the real estate agent had been forced into leasing the shop to Bryan. If she was to take anything that Royce said seriously, then the agent was someone she needed to speak to. Maybe she would know more about Bryan's possible secret life. She guessed that the real estate agency Royce had disappeared into was where she would find the agent she needed to speak to.

CHAPTER 8

As Nikki drove towards the real estate agency she hoped that she would be able to find some answers. She parked about halfway down the street, as all of the other spaces were taken. When she opened the door to the office, she found four people in the waiting room. A young man behind the front desk had a phone cradled between his ear and shoulder, while he typed frantically on a keyboard.

"That's right, the new apartments are up for lease, but you do have to sign an agreement ten days before the end of the month in order to lease it the following month. All of our agreements for those apartments must be signed ten days before."

Nikki edged her way to an empty chair and sat

down. A quick glance around the room revealed anxious faces. She guessed that whatever apartments were available were in high demand. A door swung open and a woman dressed in a lime green pants suit stepped out. Her crimson hair was cut short at the height of her cheekbones, and she wore a bright shade of pink lipstick.

"Hi everyone, thank you for your patience. We're just so busy today." She looked over the sign-in sheet on the front desk.

Nikki stood up. She knew if she didn't get the woman's attention now she might have to wait hours before she had a chance to speak with her.

"Excuse me, I just need a minute of your time."

"Do you have an appointment?" She glanced over the list in front of her.

"No, I'm sorry. I'm not here for an appointment. I just wanted to ask you a quick question." Nikki glanced at the other people waiting. "I promise I won't take up too much of your time."

"You look familiar." She narrowed her eyes as she looked her over. "Do I know you?

"I don't think so. My name is Nikki." She thrust out her hand.

"Little Nikki?" She squealed, then smiled. "I do know you!"

"You do?" Bewildered, Nikki stared at the woman.

"Well, I knew you when you were just a little thing that is. I'm Anne. I helped your parents buy their home. I was surprised to hear that they sold it." She gestured for her to follow her into her office. "Come in, we'll have to make it quick, though."

"Absolutely, no problem. Yes, they decided to head south for the warmer weather." Nikki grinned. "They are enjoying it." She followed her into the office.

"I'm so glad to hear it." Anne settled at her desk. "So, how can I help you? Are you looking to buy a place?"

"No, I'm happy with the apartment I'm in. It's tiny but it's mine." Nikki smiled. "Actually, I wanted to ask you about something that's been going around town as gossip. I thought the best way to fight it, is to consult the source."

"I'm the source of gossip?" Anne flushed and shook her head. "I doubt that."

"Me too, that's why I'm checking with you. Some people have been whispering since Bryan's death, that the only reason he got the shop instead of Royce was because you took a bribe from Bryan." Nikki looked into the woman's eyes. "Is it true?"

"Wow!" Anne's eyes widened. "Of course not! I would never take a bribe." She sighed. "I knew that this deal was going to cause me misery. The truth is, the rental should have gone to Royce, but then this man showed up at my office with mounds of legal paperwork. He insisted that if I didn't lease the place to Bryan he would ruin my entire business. Honestly, I love my work, but I don't know that much about the law, and I certainly don't have the money for a fancy lawyer. I just thought it would be easier to rent the place to Bryan and be done with it. So, that's what I did."

"What kind of paperwork?" Nikki felt her curiosity grow.

"I have copies of it." Anne stood up and walked over to her filing cabinet. As she pulled out a folder, she looked back at Nikki. "Do you think I could be in some kind of trouble with all of this? I've seen you with that detective. Has he mentioned me?"

"You have?" Nikki raised an eyebrow. "No, he hasn't, but he doesn't speak to me about his investigations. I don't think you'll be in any trouble, but if you'd like I could take copies of this paperwork to him, so he could make sure that there's nothing for you to be concerned about."

"I've been so nervous ever since Bryan was

killed." Anne set the folder down in front of Nikki. "I had such a bad feeling when that man came into my office. Maybe I should have said something to the police then." She frowned. "But I didn't have any reason to."

"It's okay, I'm sure you did the right thing. Do you remember the man's name?" Nikki opened the folder.

"It's on the inside of the folder. You can take the whole thing to him. Just do me a favor, Nikki, make sure he knows that I had nothing to do with this." She looked into the younger woman's eyes. "Please."

"Of course." Nikki stared back at Anne. "I'll tell him. I'm sure he'll get in contact with you." Nikki took the paperwork, left the agency and sat on a bench close by. She used her phone to look up the name listed on the paperwork. John Baker returned a lot of results, but it didn't take her long to find the right one. A picture matched the face of the man that she'd seen with Tim at the café, before Bryan was killed. She clicked on the picture, and it led her to a website dedicated to rants about the man. The accusations ranged from assault, to suspected murder.

This man is a criminal, he will bully and intimidate you until you feel like your only option is to give him what he wants. I don't have the proof to get him arrested, but prison is where he belongs.

Nikki raised her eyebrows as she read over the rant again. She clicked the link that led her to a profile of information about the person who posted the comment. He was a business owner based in Texas. "Wow, John really gets around." She pursed her lips and scrolled through more posts. Although people were quite angry at John, there was no solid information about what he had done. She guessed that in some way his victims were still frightened of him. Not a single rant indicated that the police were called regarding their interaction with John. Why was that? She sat back against the bench and considered the possibilities. Perhaps they were too frightened to call the police on him, but it didn't quite make sense that they would feel comfortable ranting about him on a website. Her next guess was that whatever deals they'd made with John, weren't legal. If that was the case it would explain why they hadn't reported him to the police, they didn't want to be arrested themselves.

Clearly, John was a strong suspect. What was he doing with Tim? Why was he in Dahlia at the time that Bryan was killed? She snapped pictures of the paperwork and sent them along with a link to the website she had found, to Quinn. As she tucked her phone back into her pocket she hoped that he could find something more substantial than she had.

A quick glance at her watch revealed that she only had a few more hours to try to find the perfect gift for Princess. She'd already been to all of the local pet shops and hadn't found anything just right. She recalled seeing a pet store near the gas station where Heather worked. As she drove she tried to push the murder to the back of her mind and come up with ideas for Princess' gift.

Nikki pulled into the parking lot of the pet shop, which was next to the gas station. As she stepped out of her car, Heather pushed open the door of the gas station. She headed for a motorcycle parked near the front door. As Nikki watched, she spotted a bumper sticker on Heather's motorcycle that advertised dog accessories.

"Heather!" She waved to her before the other woman could pull on her helmet.

"Not you again." She sighed as she looked over at her.

"Do you make gifts for dogs?" Nikki gestured to the bumper sticker on her motorcycle.

"Yes, I do." Heather eyed her as her upper lip curled.

"Do you have anything for small breeds?"

"I do. I make protective clothing, leashes and collars." She crossed her arms. "Why?"

"I am in desperate need of a gift by tomorrow morning. Do you have anything ready to go?" Nikki offered her friendliest smile.

"Everything's at my house. I have a wide selection." Heather tipped her head to the side. "It's only a few minutes away."

"I'd love to take a look if you'd let me." Nikki jingled her keys. "I can follow you there."

"Sure, all right." Heather climbed onto her motorcycle. "But you'll have to pick something fast, I have plans tonight."

"I can do that." Nikki walked over to her car and climbed in. She did hope she would find something for Princess, but she was also curious about Heather, and her lifestyle. She still could have been the person that killed Bryan, and she hoped that if she was, there would be some evidence to stumble across at her house.

As Nikki followed Heather towards her home, she noticed that the neighborhood was crowded with small houses, mingled with a few duplexes. While most of the yards were tidy, a few had scraggly, overgrown grass and untended gardens. Kids played on the quiet side streets, and several dogs barked as she drove past.

Heather turned into a narrow driveway and parked her motorcycle close to the house. Nikki was forced to park along the road as there was a car in the driveway that took up the remainder of the room. As she stepped out of her car, she noticed that the vehicle looked familiar to her. She tried to place where she'd seen it, but couldn't recall.

"Is that your car, Heather?" She caught up to the woman at the front door.

"No, it's my boyfriend's." She glanced over at it, then back at Nikki. "But he's out of town right now." She pushed open the front door and gestured for Nikki to follow.

"Do you have any pets?" Nikki stepped in behind her. She was distinctly aware of the risk of being alone with someone who could possibly be a murderer. However, nothing in Heather's home indicated she was a killer. Everything was just messy enough to be lived in, and decorated with bright colors, as well as endearing art pieces. The painting of a boy with a puppy that hung over the fireplace was too adorable for Nikki to look past.

"Not at the moment. My boyfriend and I are

thinking about getting a puppy in the future. It's just too much responsibility for the moment."

"I understand." Nikki followed Heather down a long hallway through the house. When she pushed open another door, Nikki was greeted by bursts of color and fluffy material. The workshop was packed with small outfits suitable for dogs of all shapes and sizes. The walls were lined with clothes of all different colors.

"Wow!" Nikki took a step back as she drank in the creativity that spread out before her. "You have an amazing talent."

"Thanks." Heather smiled some. "I'm afraid it's not enough yet to get me out of that dead-end job, but maybe one day." Her smile grew wider.

"I'm sure." Nikki touched one of the jackets and admired the material. "It's washable?"

"Yes, everything is washable and made from drool resistant materials, not to mention chew resistant." Heather wheeled in a rack of clothes. "These are all finished if you want to look through them."

"Thanks." Nikki began to sort through them, but her eyes were drawn back to a green shirt. It was long enough to go from Princess' neck to her tail. "Actually, what can you tell me about this?" She pointed it out.

"Oh, that's from my summer line. The material is waterproof and will protect the dog from the sun, plus it is light and breathable which means the dog won't get too hot. It's snug on the belly to prevent tripping, and of course it's chew resistant like the rest." Heather took the shirt down from the wall and offered it to Nikki.

"Wow, this is really amazing. I've never heard of anything like it." Nikki ran her fingertips across the material. "It's so soft."

"Yes, I make sure all of the material I use is flexible and smooth so there is no chance of rubbing or damage to the dog's coat." Heather crossed her arms as she studied Nikki. "Would you like to buy it?"

"Sure, how much?" She met the woman's eyes.

"Forty." She raised an eyebrow.

"Forty." Inwardly Nikki cringed. It was a bit more than she wanted to spend. However, the quality seemed fantastic, and she considered the price a bargain. She knew that Mrs. Whitter would appreciate it, she was always worried about Princess being out in the sun. "Okay, sold." She reached into her purse. "I'm surprised you haven't taken off with this business, you have some unique ideas, and your creations are gorgeous."

"Unfortunately, it's the name that matters. It's

hard to break into a business that's controlled by a few designers and the sponsors that are only loyal to them." Heather accepted the cash, then grabbed a pink bag from the table beside her. "I give out one of these goody bags to everyone with their first purchase. It has a few items in it, as well as a few business cards if you'd like to hand them out."

"I'd be glad to." Nikki hesitated as she studied Heather. "Did you ever show Bryan any of your stuff?"

"Yes." She narrowed her eyes. "He was not interested."

"I see. I'm sure your business will do well, Heather, keep at it, and thanks for this." Nikki tucked the shirt into the bag.

"It would be nice if it would." Heather led her back through the house. "Be sure to tell your customers about me."

"My customers?" Nikki flashed her a smile.

"You're a dog walker and pet sitter, right?" Heather locked her eyes to Nikki's.

"Uh, yes. How did you know?" She tried to recall if she'd mentioned it before.

"I do my research, too." Heather closed the door without saying another word.

Nikki stared at the closed door for several

seconds. What did that mean, that she did her research, too? Did she know that Nikki had been digging into her? Her stomach twisted as she wondered what Heather might have discovered by looking into her. She didn't exactly have anything to hide, but she was sure that there were some things that could be taken the wrong way.

CHAPTER 9

As Nikki walked back to her car, her cell phone began to ring. She paused beside her car and pulled her phone out. When she saw Quinn's name on the screen, she answered.

"Hi, Quinn." She pulled open the car door and slid inside. A quick glance back at the house revealed a figure in the front window. Was Heather watching her?

"Hey Nikki, thanks for the information you sent. We're looking into finding John, but it may take us some time, he's the slippery sort."

"That's fine." She stared at the car in Heather's driveway, and all of a sudden she remembered why it was familiar. "Quinn, did you have any luck enhancing the license plate on that car?"

"No, I guess the video quality is far too low to do anything with it. Why do you ask?" Keys tapped in the background.

"I'm at Heather's place right now." She put the phone on hands-free, slid her key into the ignition and turned the car on. The figure in the window disappeared. "I noticed a similar car in her driveway. I don't know if it's the same one, but she says it belongs to her boyfriend, who is out of town."

"It could just be a coincidence, but I can certainly look into it. Your theory is that the boyfriend was the one chasing Bryan? Why would he do that?" Quinn paused. "Wait, don't answer that, first, what are you doing at Heather's?"

"I needed a gift for Princess, and she has a side business. She makes clothing and accessories for pets. She also told me that she tried to show Bryan some of her products before and he wasn't interested. That might be more motive for her to have attacked him." Nikki sighed as she shifted the car into gear. "Quinn, I have no idea if she could have done this. But I think there is potential motive, she clearly had some animosity towards Bryan."

"Yes, she did. I'll dig into the boyfriend and see what I can find. Did she say where he is?"

"No, she didn't." Nikki eased the car onto the

road. "I'd better go, I'm driving, and I'm late to take the dogs for their afternoon walk."

"Okay, but Nikki please let me know if you're going to hang out with any more murder suspects, okay?" There was a hint of humor in his voice, but also a touch of frustration.

"I'll do my best." She smiled, then hung up the phone. Just hearing his voice had a way of boosting her mood. Or maybe she simply felt better that she'd finally bought Princess her present.

As Nikki drove, exhaustion began to set in. She hadn't gotten any sleep the night before, and now all she wanted was to curl up in bed. With several dogs waiting for her, she knew that wasn't an option. She decided to stop at the café instead for a cup of coffee to go. The parking lot was pretty full when she pulled in. Inside the café, most of the tables were occupied. She spotted a familiar face right away. Royce, with his cell phone pressed against his ear, stood a few feet away from the counter. She decided to focus on just getting her coffee. However, as she walked to the other end of the counter, Royce gravitated in her direction. Soon he was only a few steps away.

"Hi Nikki, what can I get you?" Gina smiled as she paused in front of her.

"Just a coffee to go, please." She passed a glance in Royce's direction.

"No problem. Mrs. Whitter was in here earlier, all excited about the party." Gina laughed and shook her head. "I'd say she was glowing. She wanted to tell me all about the perfect gift she bought for Princess."

"Oh, I'm so glad she found something. I know she was so worried about it." Nikki turned her attention to Gina, though she remained aware of Royce's proximity.

"She told me it's an outdoor agility course designed for small dogs. I think it sounds great, but from what she described, I'm a little worried about her setting it up herself." Gina looked towards the door and greeted a few new customers.

"I'll make sure I offer to help her. But you know Mrs. Whitter." Nikki smiled.

"That's for sure." Gina shook her head, then turned away and picked up a coffee pot.

Nikki shifted her attention back to Royce. Another waitress poured his coffee into a cup.

He impatiently drummed his fingertips on the counter as he continued his conversation on the phone.

"I am going to rent it. No one is going to play

any games with me this time." He gestured to a waitress behind the counter. "Can I get my coffee while it's hot, please?"

"Here it is, sir." She frowned as she set the cup of coffee down in front of him.

"It's about time." Royce reached into his suit jacket to pull out his wallet from the inside pocket. As he did, Nikki caught sight of a gun holstered on his hip. Her breath caught in her throat as her gaze fixated on the weapon. Bryan was shot, perhaps by the very weapon that was only a few feet away from her. She wanted to talk to him, but she couldn't get her voice to cooperate as he headed for the door.

"Nikki. Nikki?" Gina snapped her fingers in front of Nikki's face. "Are you in there? Don't you want your coffee?"

"Oh yes, sorry." Nikki watched the café door close, then turned back to look at Gina. "Thanks." She tossed some money on the counter.

"Nikki, are you okay? You look so pale." Gina frowned as she handed her a cup of coffee.

"I'm fine, thanks, but I have to go." She hurried out the door with the hot coffee burning through the thin, paper cup against her palm.

Nikki spotted Royce's car, just as it pulled away from the parking lot. She ran towards her car, but as she did the lid on her coffee cup popped open, and the hot liquid splashed across her skin.

"Ouch!" Nikki winced and grabbed the cup with her other hand. As she shook the coffee from her hand she tried to grab the car door handle, but her fingers slipped free of it and she lost her center of balance. As she stumbled forward, the coffee cup tumbled out of her other hand and splashed across the outside of her car. "Well, great!" She sighed as she stared at the puddle of coffee. When she looked up at the road again Royce's car was already gone. She pulled her phone out of her purse and called Quinn. After the third ring she heard the greeting and instructions to leave a message.

Breathlessly, she explained what she had just seen, and her suspicion that Royce was the one who killed Bryan. As she hung up the phone she wondered if the best lead in the case had just walked away. A glance at the clock on the car radio showed that she was quite late to pick up the dogs for their afternoon walk. Not all of the dogs that walked in the morning, walked in the afternoon, but she did find that some of the owners were asking her to walk them more often, which gave her a vote of confidence. Despite the fact that she spilled all of her coffee, she felt more awake than ever.

After Nikki dropped off her car at her apartment, she began to walk the neighborhood to pick up each dog for their walk. The dogs were eager to get outside. As she began to stroll towards the park, she kept her eye out for any sign of Royce. She hadn't heard back from Quinn yet, and she hoped that meant he might have already arrested Royce. Perhaps as she walked along the sidewalk, Bryan's murder was being solved. Her muscles began to relax at the thought. When her phone rang a few minutes later, she was relieved to see that it was Quinn. She answered the phone. Her mind buzzed with the anticipation of good news.

"Hi Quinn, did you get my message?"

"Yes, I did. Sorry for the delay in getting back to you, I was conducting an interview." Quinn sighed. "Not that it led me anywhere."

"I'm sorry for the interruption. Did you pick up Royce? I'm sure that he must be the killer, he's armed." Nikki steered the dogs away from a woman with a stroller. A few of the dogs were a bit too friendly to be around a little one.

"I can't pick up Royce. He has a license to carry

a concealed weapon, and when asked he provided it for examination. The bullet that killed Bryan didn't come from that gun." Quinn cleared his throat. "That doesn't mean he didn't do it. He could have access to other weapons that we don't know about. But as of now, I do not have enough proof to arrest him."

"Oh no, I really thought maybe all of this would be over." Nikki couldn't hide the disappointment in her voice.

"I know, it can be frustrating. You did the right thing by letting me know what you saw. I'm still trying to get my hands on Tim, so if you see him let me know. I've got a few patrol cars searching for him." Quinn took a deep breath. "Nikki, you have the party tomorrow to think about. Why don't you just relax and enjoy the celebration."

"Quinn, I'm sorry if all of my calls and texts are bothering you. I just really want to find out what happened to Bryan." Nikki guided the dogs through the park's entrance.

"It's not bothering me, Nikki, I want to hear everything that you have to say. But you need to stay out of this, you need to be cautious. This will be solved soon. I don't want you getting hurt."

"Thanks for the concern, but I'll be fine." She

stifled a yawn, and hoped that he didn't hear it. Yes, she was tired. Yes, she felt confused as she tried to shift her suspicion from Royce to someone new. Heather? "Is there anything new on Heather's boyfriend?"

"Although the make and model of the car do appear to match up, we can't verify with certainty that it is the same car we saw in the video. Unfortunately, it's a fairly popular vehicle. I have not been able to locate him, and Heather is not exactly being cooperative." Quinn hesitated, then continued. "I'll catch up with you later. Enjoy the rest of your day."

"You, too." Nikki hung up the phone and sighed. She was tired and annoyed that the case hadn't been solved, yet.

"Sounds like someone got under your skin." A familiar voice summoned her attention from a tree just beside the sidewalk.

Nikki jumped, startled that someone was so close without her realizing. When she looked towards the tree, she found Tim's gaze settled on her as he reclined against the thick trunk of the tree. She froze at the sight of him.

"Tim."

"Yes, it's me, and I'm glad that I wasn't the one

on the phone with you." He grinned, which caused the corners of his eyes to crinkle.

"I'm just tired." She shook her head and brushed a few strands of her hair away from her face. "It makes me a little snappy."

"I understand." He looked over the dogs. "Are they all yours?"

"No, none of them are, actually. I'm a dog walker." She smiled. "I get to borrow other people's pets."

"Oh, that sounds like a nice way to spend your time." Tim held out his hand towards Coco. "Hey there, buddy."

The German Shepherd barked and tugged at the leash as he attempted to get a good whiff of Tim's hand.

"He's a big guy, isn't he?" Tim raised an eyebrow. "Is he friendly?"

"They all are, but they're also very protective." Nikki wrapped the leashes around her hand to ensure that the dogs remained close to her.

"Do you think there's reason for them to be?" Tim gazed at her with a slight pout in his lips. "I thought we got past that."

"Tim, I don't know you at all. I am very sorry that you lost your brother, but the truth is you were in that shop when you shouldn't have been. Just because you are Bryan's brother, doesn't mean I can trust you." Nikki looked back into his eyes in an attempt to find some hint, any clue as to whether he murdered his brother.

"I told you why I was there." Tim frowned, then stood up from the tree. "Do you think I'm lying to you?"

"I think you have a shady past." Nikki ran her finger across her phone and did her best to select the redial option.

"I don't know what that has to do with anything." He shoved his hand into his pocket. "Sure, I've had a rough life, things didn't go as well for me as they did for Bryan. But I would never do anything to hurt my brother."

"I'm sure you wouldn't do anything deliberately. But sometimes people lose their cool." Nikki slipped her phone into her pocket, unsure if the call had gone through. "Tim, we're here together in this park, and Bryan is gone. All I want is the truth. You must have some idea of what happened to your brother."

"Why?" He narrowed his eyes. "Because I've had some trouble in the past? That's pretty judgmental of you. I hoped I would see you again, because you're the only person I know in town. I need your help."

"You need my help? With what?" Nikki studied him as she wondered what his intentions might be.

"I haven't been able to find Bryan's will. My mother is too sick to make the trip here to make arrangements for his burial. I need to find his will, and other papers, so that I can get all of this settled." Tim sighed and scratched his fingers back through his hair. "I've searched his apartment, but I can't find any of it. I know that you knew him, I thought maybe you would know about a storage place, or if he mentioned a special place he kept things?"

"I didn't know him very well, I'm sorry." Nikki's heart softened as she detected the desperation in his voice. He had just lost his brother, and it sounded like he was overwhelmed with the arrangements that needed to be made. "I wish I could help you."

"Do you?" Tim tipped his head to the side as he looked into her eyes. "Because you seem nervous. Is that really all because I've made a few missteps in my life?"

"No, it's because you were here before your brother was killed, with a man who has a very checkered past. I saw you in the café that morning with John. Were you two talking about Bryan?"

Her heartbeat quickened as she knew that she had just stepped into dangerous territory.

"John?" Tim cleared his throat and slipped his hand back out of his pocket. "Do you know him?"

"No, but I have looked into him, and he's not a great guy, is he?" Nikki raised an eyebrow and did her best to hide the quiver in her hands.

"I don't know him well." He shrugged and glanced towards the road, before he looked back at her. "I ran into him when I stopped at the café for breakfast. We did some business together before. That's all." He raked his eyes along the length of her. "I must have made quite an impression on you for you to remember seeing me."

"I'm just observant." She reached down and patted the top of Coco's head as he barked again. "But that still doesn't answer my question. What were you doing in the café in the first place?"

"Like I said, having breakfast." Tim chuckled, though his laughter sounded too hard to be jovial. "You're right, I came into town to see my brother. I thought we could finally get on the same page about things. I wanted to show him how much I had changed, and build a relationship with him. But before I could, someone from this town robbed me of that opportunity. And here you are, accusing me of killing my own brother?"

"I never said that." She took a step back as he leaned towards her. A few of the dogs began to growl. Coco's barking became more insistent.

"You didn't have to. I can see it in your eyes, in the way you shy back from me." He smiled some as he looked into her eyes. "You're frightened of me. But you can feel that spark between us too, can't you? What's wrong, Nikki, you've never been attracted to a bad boy before?" His smile spread into a grin.

"Tim!" Quinn called out as he closed his car door. "I've been looking for you."

Nikki's eyes widened at the sight of Quinn as he approached. His stern expression, and tense muscles made him look far different than she was used to. She realized that he had probably listened to every word of their conversation.

"Who's this?" Tim narrowed his eyes as he eyed Quinn. A second later a patrol car, with its lights flashing pulled up behind Quinn's car. "Aw, Nikki, what did you do?" He turned his attention back to her, as a quick fury bolted through his eyes. "I trusted you!"

"You just need to answer some questions," Nikki

stumbled over her words as she stepped farther back in response to Quinn's swift approach. He moved between Nikki and the dogs, and Tim.

"You don't have to answer him, Nikki." He grabbed Tim by the arm. "Don't you say another word to her. You and I need to have a conversation."

"Sure." Tim continued to stare hard at Nikki. "I know how conversations with cops end up. Congratulations, Nikki, now they're going to lock me up and throw away the key. But I guess in this town, justice is just a joke. That explains why no one is bothering to find out what really happened to my brother."

"Quinn will treat you right, Tim." Nikki bit into her bottom lip as she wondered if she'd done the right thing. With Tim's history, there was a good chance that he would be the prime suspect. But had he killed his brother?

"Nikki, enough." Quinn shot her a look of warning. "Go ahead and get the dogs home, I've got it from here."

Nikki's heart dropped as she wondered exactly what he thought of her. From the look in his eyes, it didn't seem good. Had she meddled too much in his investigation at this point? Was his patience gone?

"Sure, go on, Nikki." Tim smirked as Quinn started to lead him towards the car.

Nikki hesitated for another second, then urged the dogs along the sidewalk. With each step, she grew more frustrated. Tim had all the hallmarks of a good suspect. That was the problem. He was too good of a suspect, and it would be very easy to pin his brother's murder on him. But what if he was innocent?

CHAPTER 10

As Nikki walked each dog home, she felt her exhaustion threaten to take over. Perhaps that's why it seemed as if Quinn was upset with her, why it bothered her so much that Tim looked at her with betrayal in his eyes. She barely knew the man, and yet it upset her to think that she had hurt him.

"What you need is a nap." She rubbed her hand across her eyes and began to walk back towards her apartment.

After Nikki kicked off her shoes, and crawled into bed, she expected to fall asleep right away. Instead, she remained restless. As she tossed and turned, she couldn't escape a deep ache in her stomach. Dread, that's what it was. She squeezed her eyes shut tight and tried to block it out. Still, she felt as if she'd done something terrible. With Tim in custody, the investigation might be closed, and there was a real possibility that Bryan's killer would remain free. Of course, on the other hand, Tim might have been the one to do it. At some point the swirl of thoughts in her mind finally gave way to slumber.

When Nikki opened her eyes again, the entire house was dark. She wiped her eyes, then looked at the clock on her bedside table. It was almost eight-thirty. She'd slept quite a few hours. That ache in her stomach had become an insatiable gnawing and she realized that she hadn't had anything to eat. She made her way into the kitchen. When she opened the refrigerator to look inside she recalled that she hadn't made it to the grocery store. She didn't want to go shopping. She needed food fast.

Nikki decided to head to the café. She knew it didn't close until ten. Given the time, she decided to drive instead of walk. The streets of Dahlia were fairly empty. Most people were home getting settled on their couch for the evening. She felt out of whack with her sleep schedule, and wondered when she would get it straightened out again. She guessed she wouldn't until the murderer had been found. When she pulled into the parking lot of the café it was nearly empty. She was tempted to call Quinn for an update on Tim. He hadn't called or texted her all evening. She recalled the look in his eyes as he walked towards her and Tim in the park. Maybe he needed a break from her.

Nikki stepped into the café, and almost walked right into Gina.

"Oops, sorry." She laughed as she slid a chair back into place. "Oh, Nikki, what's wrong?" She stared into her eyes.

"Nothing. Why?" Nikki pushed her hair back from her face and realized that she hadn't brushed it.

"Honey, you look exhausted." Gina frowned.

"I just woke up, actually." Nikki shook her head. "I've got my days and nights reversed."

"Well, sit down, and I'll get you something good to eat." She headed towards the kitchen.

"I thought maybe a burger and fries would be good, if it's not too late to order that." She settled at one of the tables.

"It's not too late, but you need something better than that. I'll bring it out." She disappeared into the kitchen.

Nikki smiled to herself. There were times that

Gina didn't let her order, she would just bring her whatever she thought Nikki needed to eat. Nikki didn't mind, in fact she felt lucky to have a friend that cared about her so much. It wasn't long before she returned with a plate of pot roast, mashed potatoes, and buttered vegetables, as well as a large, fresh baked roll.

"That's a lot of food, Gina." Nikki's stomach rumbled at the sight and smell of it.

"You need to eat." She gave her shoulder a light poke. "People can't live on coffee alone."

"True. Thanks, Gina." Nikki didn't mention spilling the coffee earlier in the day.

"Allen added a little extra for you." Gina grinned referring to the cook who had a crush on Nikki.

"Thanks." Nikki smiled. "Do you have time to sit with me?"

"A few minutes." Gina settled in the chair across from her. "So, what's up with you and the great detective?"

"Quinn?" She laughed at the description. "There's nothing up."

"Oh, yes there is." Gina kicked her foot lightly under the table. "I see the way you look at him."

"You do?" Nikki groaned around a mouthful of meat. "I hope he doesn't."

"Oh honey, he looks at you the same way." She winked.

"That's not true, trust me." Nikki sighed as she took a sip of her tea. "I think he's had about enough of me."

"I doubt that." Gina looked up as the door to the café swung open. "I think someone is here to see you." She tipped her head in the direction of the door.

"Who?" Nikki followed her gaze, and found Quinn as he stepped through the door. She met his eyes accidentally, and looked away as quickly as she could. "Oh."

"Oh." Gina winked at her. "Make sure you eat." She gave Nikki a light pat on the shoulder, then headed back to the counter.

"Mind if I join you?" Quinn paused just beside her table.

"Not at all." Nikki shot him a brief smile, though she avoided meeting his eyes. "Are you hungry?"

"I actually just grabbed a sandwich at home. I was on my way back to the station, and I spotted your car in the parking lot." He sat back in his chair and released a long breath. "It's been an interesting day."

"Yes, it has." She took another bite of her food.

"So?" Quinn smiled some as he looked at her.

"So, what?" Nikki raised an eyebrow and managed to avoid his eyes once more.

"So, aren't you going to ask me for an update on the case?" His smile spread wider. "I know you can't resist."

"I know I've been pestering you." She glanced in his direction. "I'm sorry about that."

"What are you talking about?" Quinn shook his head and sat forward again. "You've given me some of the best leads in this case. How can that be pestering?"

"Earlier, it just seemed like you might have been a little annoyed with me." Nikki pushed her hair back behind her ear and dared to meet his eyes.

"I was annoyed with that scumbag Tim being anywhere near you, not with you." He tapped his hand lightly on the table.

"We don't know that he's a scumbag." Nikki frowned as she looked across the table at him. "He seemed to be really upset about his brother's death."

"Do you think so?" His eyes narrowed as he studied her. "What is your opinion of him?"

"I'm not sure exactly. But I do think he deserves a fair shake. It would be so easy to just assume that he is guilty with his background, and his presence in the area. But that doesn't prove that he is the killer." Nikki sighed and sat back in her chair.

"No, it doesn't prove it, but it does make it more likely. I have looked more into his criminal history. Many of his crimes were very violent." Quinn folded his hands on the table in front of him. "You need to be careful of him, Nikki."

"I can see why." Nikki chewed on her bottom lip as she considered the new information. "But being guilty of another crime does not make him guilty of this one."

"You seem to be very interested in him being innocent." Quinn's tone hardened just enough for her to notice it. "Are you sure you're impartial about this?"

"What does that mean?" She watched him as she felt heat fill her cheeks. "I just want to make sure there isn't a rush to judgment."

"There isn't." He held her gaze. "I don't have enough to arrest him. But he is definitely a person of interest, and I would recommend that you stay away from him. Whether or not he is the killer, he is certainly a dangerous person with a history of violence."

"I understand." She drew a deep breath, then let it out slowly. "Okay, so it's clear that Tim is a pretty good suspect. But what about Heather? Did you find out anything more about that car in her driveway?"

"Unfortunately, no. It is registered to her boyfriend, who we did confirm is out of town. We can't prove that it is the same car that was on the road with her and Bryan that night. Also, Heather has an alibi for the time that Bryan was killed. She was at work, and her manager was there with her. Royce also has an alibi, but it's not a great one. He said he was home with his wife at the time of the murder. However, he is a viable suspect because he has experience with guns, is familiar with the shop, and had some pretty serious issues with Bryan." He spread his hands out before him. "At this point yes, Tim is the best suspect. He refuses to give us any information about where John might be, how they know each other, or how he might have been involved, which makes him even more suspicious in my eyes." He leaned across the table and looked into her eyes. "How much can he care about his brother if he's not willing to give any information that might help solve the crime?"

"Maybe he just knows that John wasn't involved." She stared back at him.

"There you go defending him again." Quinn

furrowed an eyebrow as he looked at her. "What is it about him that makes you think he's so innocent?"

"I don't necessarily think that he's innocent, I just don't know that he's guilty."

"That's what I need to find out." He smiled. "I guess I'd better get back to work on this."

"Princess' party is tomorrow, I know Mrs. Whitter would love it if you were there." She watched him walk to the door.

"I'll probably be too caught up in the case, but be sure to tell Princess happy birthday from me." Quinn grinned as he started to turn away. "I don't think I've ever wished a dog happy birthday before."

"I'll be sure to pass it along." She smiled.

As Quinn left the café Nikki wondered if he would be too busy with the case, or he just wanted to create some distance between them. Perhaps he sensed what she felt for him and wanted to make it clear that he wasn't interested. Or maybe, he was just doing his job, and she was reading far too much into it. Either way, she knew the most important thing was solving the case.

CHAPTER 11

After Nikki returned to her apartment, she spent some time looking into Royce. There was good reason to suspect him. Even though the gun he carried was not the gun that killed Bryan, he might have had access to more unregistered weapons. His anger over the way Bryan managed to steal the rental space out from under him, did seem strong enough for him to cause Bryan physical harm. But that didn't prove he was the killer.

Nikki skimmed through several posts on a few different social media pages connected to Royce. Most of the comments were pleasant, if not a bit detached. However, when she came across comments regarding Bryan, Royce's entire tone shifted. The comments he left were harsh and to the point. He openly accused Bryan of stealing the shop out from under him, and indicated that he had criminal connections that made it happen. While most of his comments were left unanswered, there was one particularly threatening comment that Bryan did reply to. Nikki held her breath as she read through what may have been some of the murdered man's last words.

Royce, up to this point I have ignored your outrageous comments. However, it needs to be said that I did not do anything you are claiming. I have never and would never associate with any kind of criminal. I was told that you had backed out of your lease, perhaps you didn't have the money to cover it, or you found another space that you preferred. I'm sorry if whatever plans you had fell through and now you are upset that you did not get the shop space, however spreading lies and terrible accusations is not the way to handle your problem. Dahlia has plenty of places to rent and set up shop. Perhaps you could look into another space and move on from this. It can't be healthy for you to be this obsessed and untruthful. I wish you the best in your future endeavors.

Nikki stared at the screen, uncertain of how to take Bryan's comment. It seemed to come from a place of civility, but at the same time she could detect the anger and frustration hidden beneath it.

She noticed that Royce had not replied to that message. Had he seen it before killing Bryan? Had his denial been what sent Royce over the edge? She had very little knowledge of Royce, which made figuring out what his emotional reaction might have been, that much harder. She decided the best way to get to know him better was to take a look at his house. His address wasn't far, and she was restless. Maybe she would find a car that matched the car in the surveillance video. If she did it might point Quinn in the right direction.

As Nikki drove in the direction of Royce's house she considered what the party might be like the next day. She already knew that Mrs. Whitter would be a nervous wreck. She planned to get there early to help her set up the agility set. If she called first, she knew that Mrs. Whitter would refuse her help. But if she showed up, the stubborn woman was more likely to accept it.

Nikki was so distracted with thoughts about the party that she almost missed the house. She slowed down just before she reached it. The house number was clearly marked. She noticed a blue sedan in the driveway, as well as a red convertible. She was about to snap a picture of both license plates, when she noticed that there were two people in the driveway, nearly hidden by the shadow of a nearby tree. She sped up enough not to look conspicuous, but as she did she tried to get a good look at the two people. She recognized the man right away, it was Royce. But the woman he had his arms wrapped around was a surprise. Her eyes widened as she watched them tangle together in a passionate kiss. She nearly ran off the road but managed to straighten the car out and continue on. She hoped that neither of them noticed her presence. Yes, it was Royce in his driveway, but that was most certainly not his wife with him. In fact, it was the real estate agent, Anne.

As the pair disappeared inside the house, Nikki pulled her car to a stop in front of the next house on the street. Clearly, they were involved in an affair, but she was curious about whether they were also partners in crime. She opened her car door as quietly as she could, then closed it just as softly. She edged her way back towards Royce's house, then crept up the driveway, and along the side of the house. Once she reached the house she followed the sound of their voices towards the room they were in. It wasn't hard, as they weren't quiet. In fact, it sounded as if they were arguing. She leaned close to the window in an attempt to hear their exact words, but their voices were still too muffled for her to hear clearly. While she was focused on listening to their argument, she didn't notice the sound of another engine in the driveway, until it turned off.

The sudden lack of noise alerted Nikki to the presence of someone else. She held her breath and edged towards the rear of the house. Had she been seen? Who had pulled in? She wasn't daring enough to try to get a look at the car. As she looked for a way to escape without being seen, she heard the back door swing open. Anne ran across the back-yard, with her high heels grasped in one hand and her purse in the other. All at once Nikki put together what must have happened, Royce's wife had come home. She knew she was in just as much danger of being caught. Instead of running after Anne, she ran into the next- door neighbor's yard. She managed to get back out to the street without being spotted. As she raced in the direction of her car, she realized that maybe Quinn was right. Maybe she did take more risks than she should. Royce was a potential murderer, and more likely guilty now that she realized how much he had to hide.

Once in her car, Nikki started the engine and drove off. Whether or not she was spotted, or heard, she had no idea. A glance over her shoulder revealed that no one was following her, but that did nothing to slow down her racing heartbeat. As she turned down the next street she had to pull off to the side of the road in order to catch her breath. Royce and Anne were having an affair? She knew that could change everything. Anne had given no indication of being in a relationship with him when she spoke to her. Then again, most people didn't advertise that they were sleeping with another woman's husband. She couldn't help but wonder if they might have worked together to get rid of a man who was a thorn in both of their sides. Maybe they had concocted a plan to put an end to Bryan, so that they could get the rental space back. Perhaps Royce snapped when he read the post in which Bryan denied any association with criminals. But would Anne really help him take care of the problem? She wasn't sure.

Nikki pulled out her phone and typed out a text to Quinn about what she'd found. Just after she hit send, her phone rang. She jumped at the sound, and quickly looked out the window to see if it had drawn anyone's attention. As she answered the phone she turned the car back on.

"Hi Quinn."

"Hard at work again I see. Do I want to know how you found this information out?"

"Probably not." Nikki wiped a bit of sweat from her forehead. "Goodnight, Quinn."

"Goodnight." He sighed as he hung up the phone.

Once Nikki's head hit her pillow, she fell asleep fairly quickly. She jolted awake at the sound of her alarm the next morning. After a few seconds of fog, she realized it was the day of Princess' party. She jumped out of bed and hurried to wrap Princess' gift. Then she grabbed a banana and headed out the door. If she knew Mrs. Whitter as well as she thought she did, she guessed that the woman had already been up for a few hours to prepare for the party. She had a little time before the dogs were due for their morning walks, so she headed straight for Mrs. Whitter's. When she pulled into the driveway she noticed that it, and the front walkway had been neatly swept. All of the bushes and flower beds which were normally spotless, had been tidied up even further. She knew this was all Mrs. Whitter's handiwork as the gardener had already been at the house earlier in the week.

When Nikki knocked on the door, she prepared to face a fight about her offer of help. She heard Princess bark on the other side of the door. Then the door swung open to reveal Mrs. Whitter's slight frame.

"Oh, Nikki!" She clasped the younger woman's cheeks with her hands and gazed into her eyes. "You're just who I needed to see."

"I am?" Nikki smiled, a little nervous about Mrs. Whitter's reaction.

"Honestly, I need your help. I only have a few hours left to prepare for the party and nothing is going smoothly this morning." Mrs. Whitter thrust her thumb into the air. "I cut myself with the hedge trimmers, and I almost burned the cookies I baked for all of Princess' friends."

"I'm so sorry, but I am here to help. You just tell me what you need, and I'll do it." Nikki felt some relief at not having to battle Mrs. Whitter.

"If you could start with the agility set I bought for Princess, that would be great. I want it to be set up in the backyard so that all of the guests will be able to use it, but I'd like to add bows to each portion of it so that Princess will know that it's her birthday present." Mrs. Whitter pointed down the hall. "It's in the laundry room, you can take it right out through the kitchen door."

"Sure, no problem." Nikki smiled. If it were another dog, she might point out that a dog would have no idea what bows meant. However, she knew Princess' reaction when she saw bows. Mrs. Whitter had given her so many gifts that now she knew if there was a bow on a box, it was for her, and there was something wonderful inside. Nikki presumed that Princess must be having her breakfast because she hadn't greeted her at the door.

As Nikki walked towards the laundry room, she caught sight of Princess' bed. Its fluffy edges were tattered, as if she had been chewing on them. That wasn't something that Princess usually did. She was quite dainty when it came to the things she loved. She thought about mentioning it to Mrs. Whitter, but decided against it. She didn't want to upset her on such a special day. However, she also knew that Mrs. Whitter would not want any of her guests to see her precious pup's bed in tatters. She knew there was an extra bed in the laundry room, she would just switch them around.

Nikki grabbed the agility set, which was in a large and fairly heavy cardboard box, and the extra bed, then headed back out into the living room. She set down the agility set and the replacement bed, then reached for the old one. As she picked up the old bed, her hand closed around something lumpy inside of the material. It wasn't just in one spot, but spanned the entire ring of the bed. Curious, she began to dig into one of the holes that Princess had chewed. After a few seconds of trying she managed to get one of the lumps free from the hole. A green jewel rolled into the palm of her hand. As she stared at it stunned, and perplexed at why it would be hidden inside of the bed, Mrs. Whitter walked into the room.

"Nikki, what's that?" She walked towards her, her eyes wide.

"I don't know. I noticed that Princess had been chewing on her bed, so I thought it would be best to switch it around for her extra bed before the guests arrive. When I picked it up, I felt lumps inside of it. I dug into it, and this is what came out." Nikki held her palm out for Mrs. Whitter to see. "It must be fake. But why would anyone put that inside of a bed? Where did you get the bed from?"

"I bought it from a boutique in Maines." Mrs. Whitter narrowed her eyes as she looked over the bed. "But something isn't right." She rolled the material between two fingertips. "No this isn't right at all!"

"What is it, Mrs. Whitter?" Nikki watched as confusion spread across the woman's face.

"This isn't the bed I bought. This material is too rough for Princess. I would never let her near a bed like this. Are you playing some kind of joke on me, Nikki? Today is not the day for that!" Mrs. Whitter frowned and drew her hand away from the bed.

"No, not at all, Mrs. Whitter. This is the bed that was here when I arrived today. Like I said, when I saw it chewed up, I knew you wouldn't want your guests seeing that." She stared at the bed, and shook her head slowly. "Is it possible that you're mistaken?"

"Absolutely not." Mrs. Whitter flipped the bed over in her hands and found the tag on the bottom of it. "You see, this is from Bryan's boutique. I never bought a bed from Bryan. You know how Princess only sleeps in plush fabric. I even took in the old bed to Bryan to see if he had one with similar material, but he didn't so I never bought one." She pursed her lips as her eyes narrowed. "To think that my poor Princess has been sleeping in this heap of trash for who knows how long. How awful. No wonder she chewed it up."

"I don't think she chewed it because of the material, Mrs. Whitter, I think she was trying to get to these gems." Nikki frowned as she felt the ring of the bed again. "There are lots more inside. Why would anyone put them inside of a dog bed?"

"I have no idea." Mrs. Whitter crossed her arms. "But I certainly don't have time for this today."

"Unless." Nikki's eyes widened as she gazed down at the green stone in her hand. "Mrs. Whitter, what if they're real?"

"Real?" She stared back at her with disbelief. "They couldn't possibly be, could they?"

"Why else would someone go to all of the trouble of hiding them inside a dog bed?" Nikki raised an eyebrow as her thoughts began to churn. She recalled how Bryan refused to sell her the key rings with the green gems in them. "Oh no, Mrs. Whitter, I'm afraid this could be quite serious."

"What do you mean, Nikki?" She pressed her hand against her chest. "I can't take any trouble today. You know how important it is to me."

"I do know that, and I'm sorry, Mrs. Whitter. But I think these gems are real, and I think Bryan has been smuggling them. As long as they are here, you won't be safe, and neither will your guests." She gripped the bed tightly. "We need to get the police involved right away."

"Real?" Mrs. Whitter stammered as she continued. "You think Bryan had something to do with this?"

"The other day, when he was here, did you leave him alone at all?" Nikki slid the emerald back into the bed with the others, placed the bed on the floor and began to pace slowly back and forth.

"Yes, I did, for a few minutes. But he wouldn't do something like this, Bryan was a good man, and—"

"And he insisted that you return the collar with the gems in it, remember?" Nikki snapped her fingers. "He must have known it had real jewels in it."

"If he did, then why would he leave the bed here? Why would he want to hide the jewels in my home?" Mrs. Whitter's voice shook. "None of this makes any sense."

"You're right, Mrs. Whitter, but I know one thing for certain. We need to call Quinn." Nikki reached for her phone, but realized she'd put it down on the dryer when she was in the laundry room. She'd left it behind as she carried the agility set and bed out of the laundry room. "Let me just get my phone."

Nikki turned back towards the hallway to get it, and came face to face with John, the conman who had strong-armed Anne into giving Bryan the lease for the shop.

CHAPTER 12

The moment Nikki saw John, her heart jumped into her throat. She found it hard to swallow, or take a full breath. She stared straight into his eyes.

"What are you doing here?"

"What am I doing here?" He smiled as he looked from her to Mrs. Whitter. "I'm here to get back what belongs to me."

"Nothing here could possibly belong to you." Mrs. Whitter crossed her arms, her voice strong as she spoke.

"Oh, I disagree." John rested his hand on his hip, just above a gun tucked into his belt. "You see, I thought perhaps my merchandise was at the shop. But it wasn't. Then I began to trace the movements

Bryan made before his unfortunate demise. I noticed that he made a stop at this house. But why? No one around town indicated that you were friends. Bryan had no reason to be here." He looked between the two women again. Just then, Princess bolted in from the other room, and began to bark.

"I don't know what you're talking about." Nikki's heart raced. She could guess what he was looking for, but she knew that if she gave him the jewels, he wouldn't hesitate to kill them both.

"Jewels. Emeralds, to be exact." He eyed the dog as she barked and bounced back and forth on her feet. "Shut that thing up."

"Don't talk to her that way." Mrs. Whitter gasped and scooped Princess up into her arms.

"We don't have any emeralds." Nikki stepped between him and Mrs. Whitter. "You're mistaken. If you leave now, we won't call the police. We'll just consider it a misjudgment."

"I'm not going anywhere, sweetheart." John pulled his gun from his waistband. "And if you don't shut that dog up, I'll shut her up!"

"No!" Mrs. Whitter shrieked.

"Stop, please!" Nikki used her body to block Mrs. Whitter and Princess. "Please, just calm down.

If you calm down, she'll calm down. She's just trying to protect her."

"That little thing!" John sneered. "Give me the emeralds!" He waved his gun in the air.

"Wait, please." Nikki knew she had to think fast. If he was pushed, he would just kill them all, then use the time to search the place. He might never find the emeralds, but what difference would that make? She looked over at Mrs. Whitter, who trembled from head to toe as she tried to quiet Princess. She had to find a way to get him away from them. As long as they were together, Mrs. Whitter was at risk. "Listen, I don't know where the emeralds are, and neither does Mrs. Whitter. But you said it's Bryan that stole them from you?"

"Yes, he did, and I think you're lying to me." John pointed the gun directly at Nikki. "A bullet might teach you not to."

"Don't!" Nikki gasped as she stared at the barrel of the gun. She tried to think of a way to delay him from pulling the trigger. "The emeralds, they're not here. But I think I know where they are."

"You do?" He lowered the gun a few inches. "Where?"

"I saw Bryan digging in the woods. I thought it was strange, but it wasn't my business, so I just kept walking. But I know where he was digging. I bet he hid them there. I can take you to them." Nikki's heart pounded so hard that she was sure he could hear the sound of it.

"Where are they? Just tell me." He took a step towards her, his eyes narrowed.

"I can't describe it. But I can take you there." Nikki drew a deep breath in an attempt to control her fear.

"You'll tell me where they are right now!" He grabbed her hard by the shoulder and shoved her out of the way, then trained his weapon on Mrs. Whitter. "Or she dies!"

"No, don't!" Nikki screamed as Mrs. Whitter gasped in fear. "She doesn't know where the emeralds are. Only I do. If you do anything to hurt her, I won't tell you. You can kill us both, but you will never find those emeralds." Her stomach clenched in terror. Would he know that she was lying? Would he shoot them both out of spite?

"This is ridiculous." He turned the gun back towards her. "I have ways of making you talk." He frowned. "But I'm short on time."

"Then it's simple. Just let me take you to the emeralds. I will show you exactly where they are, as long as you promise that Mrs. Whitter is safe. She has to stay here, with Princess." Nikki glanced at Mrs. Whitter to find that her face had gone pale, and she looked as if she might faint.

"Sure, I'll leave them here to call the police. You must think I'm plain stupid." He rolled his eyes.

"No, you can lock her in the laundry room. There's a lock on the outside of the door. There's nothing inside, no alarms, no phone lines, nothing."

"What about cell phones?" John asked.

"Her phone is on the table." Nikki pointed at the phone on the hall table as they walked past. She tried to keep her voice steady. "Mine is still in my car. She won't be able to call anyone." She gestured to the door in the hallway that led to the laundry room. "Please, if you lock her in the room, then I will have your emeralds in your hands in no time."

"It's not exactly going to be easy to haul the two of you around." He ran his free hand along his chin as he considered it. Then he gestured to Mrs. Whitter with his gun. "Go on, get in there."

"Nikki, no you can't go with him!" Mrs. Whitter gulped as she inched towards the laundry room. "You won't be safe!"

"It's okay, Mrs. Whitter. Please, just do what he says. You and Princess will be safe in there." She locked her eyes to Mrs. Whitter's. She had no idea if

Mrs. Whitter would use her phone to call for help, or even remember it was in the laundry room. But she knew it was their only hope.

"You'd better not harm her!" Mrs. Whitter shouted at John.

"Sure, whatever, just get in there." He gave her shoulder a light shove towards the door.

"Don't hurt her!" Nikki demanded.

"Calm down, she's fine." He rolled his eyes again, then closed the door the moment Mrs. Whitter was inside the laundry room. He turned the lock. Then he dragged a kitchen chair over to the door and shoved it underneath the knob. "There." He turned back to Nikki. "Now, we have some business to attend to." He pointed the gun at her. "Are you going to cooperate? Because if you cause me any trouble, I can have my partner here in seconds to finish off the old lady and her dog, too."

"I will do anything you say." Nikki nodded. "I just want them to be safe."

"Don't give me any reason to change my mind then." He gave the door a swift kick, which caused Princess to yelp and growl.

"I won't." Nikki's chest tightened with fear. She knew that eventually he would figure out that there were no emeralds in the woods, and at that point her life would probably be over. But she hoped she'd bought both herself and Mrs. Whitter enough time to survive, that was if the shock and trauma weren't too much for Mrs. Whitter's heart to take.

"Good girl." He grabbed her by the arm and pulled her towards the front door. She felt the barrel of his gun dig into her side and knew with certainty that he wouldn't think twice about pulling the trigger.

Panic pumped through Nikki's veins with each step she took outside of the house. She didn't know if her plan would work, she hadn't exactly had time to think it through. Her only goal was to get him away from Mrs. Whitter and Princess. Now she wondered if she should have told him the truth about the emeralds. Maybe he would have let them all go. She doubted it, but it might have been better than whatever was about to happen.

"Please, don't hurt them. She doesn't know anything about any of this." Nikki spoke loudly, hoping that someone passing by might hear her, though she knew it was unlikely.

"Quiet!" John pushed her roughly down the driveway. A black sedan that must have belonged to him was parked on the street. He gestured to the driver's side door.

"Get in, you're driving."

Nikki opened the door, her senses heightened by the panic that rushed through her. She guessed that once she was inside she would never be able to escape him. A quick look around revealed just how isolated she was. Mrs. Whitter's house was so far back from the road, and separated by plenty of land from her neighbors. Even if Nikki screamed, she knew it was unlikely that anyone would hear her.

"Now!" John barked at her.

"Yes, sorry." She opened the door and slid into the driver's seat.

John sat in the passenger seat, then handed her the keys. As she turned on the car, she wondered if he was Bryan's killer. It appeared as if he was capable of murder, and obviously Bryan was somehow involved with these emeralds. But if he wanted the emeralds so bad, would he have killed Bryan? She wasn't sure. As she drove down the driveway, it gave her little comfort to think that he might not be Bryan's murderer. That didn't mean that he wouldn't be hers.

Nikki did feel some relief that she had gotten him away from Mrs. Whitter, but she wondered who his partner was. Tim? Was he the type of person who could kill an elderly woman? She wanted to believe he wasn't, but after what Quinn had to say about him, she guessed he might be. Her heart pounded as she tried to think of a way to escape. She did her best to drive on the main roads as she hoped that someone might realize that she was in trouble and stop them. Her thoughts traveled to Quinn. She knew that in some way he would blame himself if she ended up dead. It wouldn't be his fault, but he was the kind of man that would take responsibility for it. She hated the thought of him being hard on himself over her mistake. Maybe if she had locked the door after she came in the house, he wouldn't have gotten inside. She couldn't honestly recall if she had locked it or not. But she knew deep down, that it wouldn't really have made a difference either way. She did all she could do to protect Mrs. Whitter, but she was terrified that it wouldn't be enough.

"Where are you going?" John barked at her and drew her back to reality.

One glance in the direction of the gun that he pointed at her, reminded her how dire her situation was. She felt a rush of fear wash over her, and regret. She'd never even had the chance to tell Quinn how she felt about him. For a second, she entertained the thought of crashing the car.

"Answer me!" John growled. "You said that it was in the woods, there are no woods in this direction!"

"We're almost there." Nikki shuddered as her hands tightened on the steering wheel. "I'm sorry, I'm not used to having a gun pointed at me."

"Trust me, sweetheart, having it pointed at you is better than what I plan to do next if you don't get me to those emeralds!" His voice raised, and he leaned closer to her, but before he could follow through, his cell phone rang. "What is it?" He growled into the phone. After a moment, his voice raised even further. "This is one big, fat mess! Be there in five minutes!" He hung up the phone, then pointed the gun directly at Nikki. "Turn left at the next intersection."

"But the gems aren't that way." Her heart lurched.

"Do what I say or you can spend the rest of the ride in the trunk." He released the safety on the gun.

"Okay, yes I will." Nikki squeezed her eyes shut for just a second, then switched on the turn signal.

One good bump in the road might set the gun off. She had to be careful. As he directed her where to go she wondered what had changed. Did he know that she was lying? Who was he on the phone with? The questions swirled in her mind as she wondered if Mrs. Whitter had found her cell phone in the laundry room. She could only hope, otherwise no one would even know she was missing. A brief glance in the direction of the clock on the dashboard revealed that she was late to pick up the dogs for their morning walk. Most of the owners were out when she picked up the dogs, they probably wouldn't notice that she didn't show up to get them.

"Turn right here, and keep going straight." He frowned as he stared at her, then turned his attention to the windshield.

Nikki's heart sank as she realized that they were headed out of town. Wherever he was taking her, she had a feeling he had no intention of ever bringing her back. Tears began to prick at the backs of her eyes as she tried to steady her emotions. Breaking down would not help her to escape, though at this point she didn't think there was any way to escape.

CHAPTER 13

"Where are we going?" Nikki stole a glance in John's direction, though barely turned her head to do so. Each time she saw the gun, her panic increased.

"Just drive." He cleared his throat and settled back in the passenger seat.

Nikki tightened her grip and considered her options. If she tried to crash the car, the gun would go off, and she might not survive it. If she tried to jump out, she would likely hit the road too hard. She began to edge the speed of the car down enough that she might survive a jump out. He didn't notice at first as he continued to stare hard through the windshield. As the car slowed down further, he looked over at her, then at the speedometer.

"What are you doing?" He snapped at her. "Why are you slowing down?"

"I can't see." Nikki sniffled as she gripped the steering wheel tight. "I'm so scared, I can't see, clearly. I'm trying not to cry."

"You listen to me!" John lunged so close to her that she winced and the car swerved slightly to the left. "You should be scared! If you do anything to draw attention to us, I will make sure that you don't ever step out of this car, understand?"

"I understand." Nikki gulped and sped the car back up. As her heart slammed against her chest she realized that everything she did from this moment on was a risk. However, she also knew that when they reached their destination, she would likely not be set free.

After driving about ten miles out of town, he pointed out a street for Nikki to turn down. The farther she drove down it, the more desolate it became. The long road led to an abandoned building, perhaps once a warehouse, where a motorcycle was parked. Her stomach twisted as she tried to work out who John had spoken to on the phone. Was it Tim? Was it Heather?

"Park right there." John pointed to an area not far from the motorcycle. "Don't bother trying to scream, there's nothing around here. I scoped it out well." He shot her a look of warning.

Nikki could only nod as she put the car into park. He snatched the keys out of the ignition.

As Nikki looked through the windshield, she saw Tim walk towards the car. Her heart dropped. She thought he was innocent. Tim seemed puzzled, then his expression darkened.

"What is she doing here?" Tim paused at the passenger side window. "Why did you bring her?"

"I told you I would get the emeralds no matter what it took. I went back to that old lady's house to look for them again." John popped the door open, but kept his gun trained on Nikki.

"I told you I already searched the house!" Tim growled. "The emeralds weren't there!"

"But you had to rush, you were interrupted."

"It doesn't matter, they weren't there." Tim raised his voice. "What have you done now? Why did you bring her?"

"She told me she knows where the emeralds are. We were on our way to get them, when you decided to call an emergency meeting!" John scowled at Tim. "This has been one big mess from the start. Now, I'm going to start cleaning it up."

"She doesn't have the emeralds!" Tim balled his

hands into fists at his sides. "There's no way she does! She would have turned them in to the police!"

"She said she saw Bryan burying something in the woods." John frowned as he looked over at Nikki. "She'd better not be lying, or she's going to pay the price."

"I'm not!" Her voice trembled as she spoke. She didn't sound convincing, even to her own ears. As she looked past John at Tim, she wondered if there was some shred of decency within him that would keep her safe.

"She's lying, you idiot. She's just trying to keep herself alive!" Tim slammed his hand against the top of the car. "I never should have gotten involved with you!"

"Well, now you are." John shifted his weapon from Nikki to Tim. "Either you tell me why you called me here, or you're going to be part of the mess that I need to clean up."

"I want to know the truth." Tim's shoulders straightened as he stared at the larger man.

"This isn't the time." John stepped out of the car, though he shot a look of warning back in Nikki's direction. "The only thing we should be focused on right now is finding the emeralds. You interrupted me in the process of getting them."

"That's crazy, she doesn't have any idea where those emeralds are." Tim rolled his eyes. "You should just let her go."

Nikki sighed with relief. Maybe she wasn't so wrong about Tim after all. He seemed eager for John to release her.

"Let her go?" John chuckled. "There's no way I'm doing that. She knows too much. If you're right and she doesn't know where the emeralds are, then she's useless to us."

"John!" Tim glared at him. "You told me that no one was going to get hurt!"

"I don't care what I told you. You knew what you were getting into. Things are out of hand, because of your idiot brother, and we have to handle it. No actually, you have to handle it." John held his gun out to Tim. "You made this mess, now you're going to take care of it. If you don't, then you become part of the mess I need to clean up, understand me?"

"John, this is crazy. Like you said, we have to find those emeralds." Tim shook his head. "Why waste our time on this?"

"I'm not wasting my time. I'm going back to that old woman's house, and I'm going to turn it upside down. If I don't find the emeralds, then I'll move on to every house in Dahlia. I will find what I'm looking for, no matter what it takes." John pushed his gun into Tim's hand. "You need to hurry up with your task, so you can help me look for them."

"All right, all right. Fine." Tim closed his hand around the gun and looked past John into the car.

Nikki looked away as she noticed his attention on her. Terrified that John would hurt Mrs. Whitter after all, she wondered if there was any way to stop him. At the moment, she couldn't think of one.

"Give me the keys to the bike." John held out his hand.

"Go easy on it." Tim tossed him the keys. Then he took the car keys from John. As he walked around to the driver's side of the car, Nikki held her breath.

"Get out." He pulled open the driver's side door.

"What?" Nikki stared up at him. "Tim, please."

"Get out of the car!" Tim demanded as John gunned the engine of the motorcycle. He took off down the long road.

Alone with Tim, Nikki had no idea if she would survive the next few minutes. She eased her way out of the car as her body trembled.

"Up against the car." He gave her a light shove.

"Tim, please, you don't have to do this."

"Quiet." Tim grabbed her hands and tied them behind her back with something that felt like a cord. Then he walked her around the car. For a second, she thought he might put her in the trunk. Instead he pushed her down in the passenger seat. As he buckled her seat belt, she hoped that meant that he wanted to keep her alive. "I'm sorry about this, Nikki. I really am."

Tim walked back around the car and climbed into the driver's seat. As the engine started, Nikki's heart sank. Any hope she had that he would let her go, vanished. She closed her eyes and hoped that by now Mrs. Whitter was safe, and Quinn was looking for her.

After several minutes of driving in silence, Nikki got the idea that Tim didn't have a particular destination. She glanced over at him, and noticed the stress that deepened the lines in his face. It seemed to her that he was tense over more than just the missing emeralds.

"I'm sorry about your brother." Nikki spoke tentatively, unsure how he would react to the sound of her voice.

"Me, too." Tim's jaw rippled, and he kept his gaze on the road.

"Were you close?" Nikki softened her voice as she sensed that his grief was raw.

"I don't want to talk about it." He veered the car into another lane, then stepped on the gas.

"Sorry." She wobbled in her seat, unable to brace herself with her hands tied behind her back. "You don't have to do this, Tim. You can trust me not to say anything."

"Right." Tim flashed her a brief smile. "You're just going to forget all about being abducted?" He shook his head and turned his attention back to the road.

"I will, I promise, Tim. I will." Nikki squirmed in her seat in an attempt to look at him, but he kept his focus on the road. As they drove along she tried to untie the rope. "I know you don't want to do this. I know that you're not a killer."

"You're wrong. I am." Tim turned off the main road. "Bryan is dead because of me." He turned down another road, that paralleled farmland, and woods.

"You can still do something about it." Nikki took a sharp breath as she wondered if his words were a confession. Had he really killed his brother? "Go to the police."

"You're crazy." He turned down another road, and she noticed that the pavement disappeared. As the car rolled along the dirt, her heart sank. This was where he was headed the whole time. He had a plan for her, and it didn't include returning her safely to her apartment.

"Please, Tim, think about what you're doing." Nikki began to panic more as he pulled the car to a stop on the side of the road. He leaned across the car and untied the cord from around her wrists.

"I have thought about it. I've thought about it from the moment that I got involved with John again. When I got out of jail, I thought I owed him something. I got arrested and he paid an attorney to help me get out. About a month ago he came to me about the emeralds. He needed a way to get them out of the country." Tim shrugged as his eyes widened. "It seemed like such a simple thing to do. I knew that Bryan wanted to open a shop, and that he would be shipping some products to customers outside the country. I was sure we could find a way to use that." He closed his eyes and leaned his head back against the seat. "I couldn't have known that things would get this out of control."

"No, you couldn't," Nikki said gently. "I know that you loved your brother. I know that you never meant for any of this to happen."

"I didn't." Tim opened his eyes and looked into hers. "But once I was involved with John, there was no way out. He set it up so that Bryan would get the shop space he needed to open his business. Bryan had no idea what was going on, until I showed up." He lowered his eyes. "You should have seen the look on his face when he saw me. I thought maybe he would be happy, but he wasn't. I tried to get him to volunteer to be involved in the smuggling, but he refused. He insisted he wanted to run a clean and legal business and that he didn't want anything to do with me or John."

"That must have upset you." Nikki chewed on her bottom lip. "You can tell me what really happened, Tim, I'm listening."

"I don't know what happened!" He shook his head. "That's the worst part of all of this. John insists that he didn't kill Bryan, but I don't know! I pulled Bryan into this mess, and eventually he complied. He helped me smuggle the emeralds in his products out of the country. I think he did it to protect me, because I told him that John would kill me if he didn't follow through. For a week, all was well. Then all of a sudden, he decided he couldn't do it anymore. John found out, he came to Dahlia. I tried to talk some sense into Bryan, I warned him that John was a dangerous man. He said that was why he needed out. He'd made a mistake and sold a collar with some of the emeralds to Mrs. Whitter. He got the emeralds back, but what if he hadn't? He couldn't live in fear. John would have gone after him." He rubbed his hand across his forehead and groaned. "He was such an idiot!" He punched the steering wheel. "All he had to do was give all the emeralds to John, but he refused, he said he didn't have them. I think he thought John wouldn't harm him until he had the emeralds. When I left the shop, he was still alive. But as I was riding away, I heard a gunshot. I heard it." He drew a sharp breath. "Someone walked right in that shop after I left and killed my brother, and I did nothing to stop it!"

"I'm sorry, that is heartbreaking, and it's going to take some time for you to get through that, Tim." Nikki's mind spun with the information he gave her. He wasn't a murderer, she wanted to believe him. He might have put his brother in danger, but maybe he wasn't the one that pulled the trigger. That meant that there really could be a spark of good inside him. "You can't do anything to change that now. But you can change this moment. You can make a good decision right now. One that your brother would be proud of, that he would encourage you to make."

"Keep quiet." He groaned again, then opened the car door. "There's nothing I can do. Either I will do it, or John will. He's going to kill me, too, if he doesn't find those emeralds."

"I can help you with that." She shifted in the car seat, her hands finally free of the cord, still ached from being tied. "I know where the emeralds are."

"Don't lie to me." Tim sighed as he looked over at her. "I know that you have no idea where they are."

"No, I do." She locked her eyes to his. "I lied to John, you're right. I lied to him because I wanted to protect Mrs. Whitter. I had to get him away from her."

"You lied to him about where the emeralds are, but you know where they are?" Tim pulled his car door shut as he stared at her. "Are you serious?"

"Yes, I am." Her stomach churned. She knew that if she led him back to Mrs. Whitter's house and she hadn't found her phone, then she would be putting her friend in danger, again. But if she had found the phone, then the police might be right there waiting for them. But she couldn't take the risk. She would pretend that the emeralds were close to Mrs. Whitter's house, buried in the park, then if the police were in the area hopefully they would see her. "I can take you to them, Tim."

"Why would you do that?" He studied her. "Why would you tell me where they are?"

"Because I want to live, Tim. I believe you don't want to hurt us. We can make a deal." She bit into her bottom lip and held her breath as she expected him to refuse.

"What kind of deal?" Tim settled back in the driver's seat.

"I will take you to the emeralds, if you promise to let me and Mrs. Whitter go. Mrs. Whitter never saw you, she has no idea that you were involved. As far as she knows, John was the only one behind all of this. I'll give you the emeralds, and you can take off. The police will have their criminal, and lock up John. He won't be able to come after you. You can start a new life somewhere fresh, somewhere tha you can forget everything that happened here." S held his gaze as her heart pounded. "You can person who I know you really are inside. have to do is agree, and within an hour y your way."

"This is just another trick." Tim frowned, but narrowed his eyes with interest.

"It isn't, Tim. If I'm telling the truth, then you'll have your emeralds, and your escape. Like you said, John is just going to kill you, too. Right?" She raised an eyebrow. "What do you have to lose?"

"Nothing, I suppose." He slid his hand along the steering wheel. "If this is some kind of game, you're going to regret it."

"Oh, it's no game. As long as Mrs. Whitter and I go free, I can assure you, you will have all of the emeralds you are looking for." Nikki felt some relief as he started the engine. She'd just bought herself a bit more time. But would it be enough?

CHAPTER 14

Nikki directed Tim back into town, though she did her best to be evasive as to where they were actually going. She made sure that he took a road that went past the police station. As they neared it, her heartbeat quickened. She knew she only had one chance at this, and if she didn't take it, she might never have another one. As he drove past the police station, she grabbed the steering wheel and tugged it hard in the direction of a group of signs.

"What are you doing?" Tim shouted as he struggled to regain control of the car. It careened into the signs, despite his best efforts. As it crashed through them, Nikki braced herself against the dashboard.

Her entire body bounced and lurched in reaction to the collision. She drew a deep breath as pain shot through her legs and wrists. The crash didn't cause as much damage as she hoped it would. As Tim started to back the car up, she reached for the door handle. The lock clicked shut before she could open it.

"Don't you even try it." Tim snarled at her as he stepped on the gas. The car flew across the road in reverse. He slammed on the brakes, which caused Nikki to crash into the dashboard again. As her vision blurred with panic and pain, she heard the sound of sirens. At least her plan had partially worked. The crash had drawn the attention of a police officer. The patrol car bolted after them. As its engine roared she found some comfort in the thought that she was about to be rescued. But as Tim navigated the streets and sharp turns, she realized that she may have underestimated him. He wove through thick traffic and then cut down a side street, losing the police car for several seconds. When the flashing lights and sirens returned, he again executed several sharp turns, and cut off a line of traffic at a green light. She squeezed her eyes shut as she anticipated the sound of shattered glass and twisting metal. Instead, he sailed right through the intersection and made another hard turn followed by a quick succession of turns that led him deeper into a heavily populated neighborhood. Only when she began to relax did she realize that she could no longer hear the sirens. Her heart sank.

"What did that do?" Tim cut a glance in her direction. "Huh? What did it do?"

Too frightened to speak, she stared through the windshield. He had lost the police officer. No one knew where she was, or who she was with, or even that she was missing, aside from Mrs. Whitter. Her best guess was that Mrs. Whitter hadn't found the phone. She was sure that if she had, Quinn would have the entire police force out looking for her. Since that didn't appear to be the case, she was quite certain that he didn't even know she was gone. She stared through the window, hoping to catch a glimpse of flashing lights. She strained to hear any hint of a siren. With every second that passed, her panic increased. At this point, she felt as if the only way out was to jump out of the car. The lock was still in place. But Tim was distracted with driving and might not notice if she unlocked it and opened the door. She shifted her body in the seat to block her actions, and managed to get the lock up. A quick assessment of their speed warned her that she might not survive hitting the road. There were also other cars around them that she might get struck by in the process. But anything had to be better than being alone with Tim as he stewed in his betrayal and anger. She gritted her teeth, then did her best to distract him. As long as he wasn't looking at the door, she thought she could get it open before he discovered that it was unlocked.

"Tim, please, just let me go! Where are you taking me?" Nikki grabbed desperately at the handle of the passenger side door.

"Enough!" He pushed the lock button, then glared at her. "If you do that again I'll make things a lot worse for you." As a car blared its horn at him, he focused his attention on the road again. "John is right. I need to listen to him, and take care of things, instead of letting things get any more out of hand."

Nikki's heart dropped at the thought of him listening to John. There would be no way to convince him that she knew where the emeralds were now. He would never believe her again. She cringed as she wondered how she had ever thought he was a good person. Was her radar so off that she didn't know when someone was a violent criminal?

She stared hard out the window in an attempt to calm herself. It didn't take long before she recognized the direction he headed in. Right back to the dirt road.

"Tim, this is a mistake." Nikki forced the words out, despite the fear that threatened to paralyze her.

"The only mistake I made was ever trusting you. I never should have believed you. You made a fool of me. I really thought we could end this without it getting even worse, but I was wrong." He turned onto the dirt road.

Nikki closed her eyes and held back tears. Maybe if she had followed through with her promise, and given him the emeralds, maybe he would have let her go. But she couldn't risk taking him back to Mrs. Whitter's house. Maybe it had been the wrong choice, but it was too late to change it now. She'd broken any chance of trust between them, and motivated him to follow through with his orders. As the knowledge of what was about to unfold set in, she felt defeated. The car came to a stop. He turned off the engine. Silence blanketed the car as neither of them moved a muscle. She wondered what ran through his mind. Did he regret the choices he'd made that led him to this moment? She certainly did.

Without looking at Nikki, Tim pushed the door open and stepped out of the car. It struck her as she watched him walk around the front of the car to the passenger side, that she might never know who killed Bryan. It could have been John, it could have been Royce, it could have even been Heather. It could be the person who pointed a gun at her through the passenger side window. Tim used his free hand to open the door.

"Get out." He held the door open.

Nikki clenched her teeth and willed herself not to scream. No one would be able to hear her, and she didn't want to give Tim the pleasure of hearing it. Did he take pleasure in this? She dared a look into his eyes, and found something molten and dark there. She couldn't place exactly what it was. But none of it looked like mercy.

"You're better than this, Tim. I know you are. You loved your brother. Don't you want to find out what really happened to him? I can help you with that." Her voice trembled, but with each word she spoke it got stronger. "I can get the detective working the case to—"

"No." Tim released the safety on the gun as he pointed it at her. "It doesn't matter. He's gone. That's all that matters. Nothing can bring him back, and nothing can change the fact that it was my fault. This is who I am, Nikki. It's who I've always been. Fighting it was the only stupid choice I ever made. Now, get out." He reached into the car and grabbed her roughly by the arm.

As he jerked her out of the seat, hot fear seized every nerve in her body. Alarms rang deep in her senses. Her knees threatened to buckle, but she managed to remain on her feet.

He gave her a light shove so that he could step behind her.

"Walk." He gestured to the woods in front of them.

"Please, Tim, don't do this." She didn't move her feet an inch.

"Walk, or I will drag you." He pointed the gun at her. "It's your choice."

Nikki forced her feet to move. The last thing she wanted was to encourage him to pull the trigger.

"I was supposed to walk my dogs today. They're probably all upset about not getting out." She shivered as she heard him step on a twig behind her. He followed so close that she could smell his cologne. "Their owners are going to be looking for me."

"Lots of people can walk dogs, don't worry." Tim gave her a light push. "Keep going."

"I guess I never thought it would end like this. There's someone I care so much about, I guess, if I'm honest, I'm in love with him." Nikki glanced over her shoulder. "I haven't even had the courage to tell him."

"I'm sorry about that." Tim moved her along with another light push. "But you're probably saving yourself some pain. True love doesn't even exist."

"I don't believe that." Her heart pounded harder with every step she took. "I've loved him since I was just a teenager."

"Sure." He grabbed her shoulder to stop her. "That's far enough."

"Tim please, don't do this." She released a slow breath as she prepared herself for what would happen next.

"Quiet!"

Nikki could feel his presence behind her. She knew that he still hesitated to pull the trigger. As much as he wanted to be the bad guy, he just didn't have it in him. The sound of a motorcycle made her jump. She sensed Tim take a few steps away from her, as someone plodded through the woods in their direction. She didn't dare to turn around. She knew who it was.

"What's going on here?" John demanded as he crossed the distance between them. "Tim, I told you to take care of this, and you still haven't?"

"She said she knew where the emeralds were." Tim frowned as he looked over at John. "I thought she was telling the truth, but it turns out it was just another one of her lies."

"And you fell for it? You told me she didn't know where they were." He ran his hand back through his hair. "Every time I start to think you've grown a brain, you show me you haven't."

"Keep quiet! You thought she had the emeralds, first! You're the one who brought her into this in the first place!" Tim turned to face him.

Nikki heard Tim's shoe twist in the dirt. She felt his attention shift from her and became aware that the gun was no longer pointed in her direction. This was her chance, her last chance, and it might be the last decision she ever made.

"You're so stupid." John scowled.

"You tell me right now!" Tim aimed the gun straight at John's face. "You tell me what you did to my brother!"

"Tim, I told you, I had nothing to do with that." John smiled and held up his hands. "Relax man."

"Liar! You're lying to me!" Tim growled and lunged forward another step.

Nikki took this as her cue. She felt her legs propel her forward without even instructing them to. Her entire body came alive with a pressing need to escape. She knew that at any second she could pay the price for her decision to run with a bullet in her back. She just hoped that the two men behind her were too involved in their own argument to notice her escape. Each time her foot landed on the ground, she felt a stronger sense of freedom. She was going to make it, she could sense it. Her blood pumped with such intensity that she could hear it.

"You did it! You promised me you wouldn't. I told you how much he meant to me. He was my brother, John! My brother!" Tim still had the gun trained on John.

"Of course, I killed him, you idiot! Of course, I did! He stole from me! He had to be taught a lesson, and so do you!"

Nikki glanced back in time to see John attempt to wrestle the gun from Tim. "You're letting her get away! She's going to ruin everything!"

Nikki gulped as she heard the focus turn on her. She knew that if she didn't get to the next patch of trees, she wouldn't stand a chance of getting away unscathed. With all of the strength she had within her she lengthened her strides and hoped it would be enough to get her past their line of fire. Just as she reached the tree line, she heard a bullet tear through the air. It was followed by the sharp pain of a solid force colliding with her side.

CHAPTER 15

As Nikki's head spun and she collapsed to the ground she was surprised at the strange sensation of being hit with a bullet. She thought that it would have hurt more. Her shoulder struck the dirt hard. In that instant she realized that she was pinned down. Had one of them been able to catch up with her that fast? Had she been running far slower than she first thought? She struggled in his grasp. As she tried to wedge her knee into any tender area she could find, he grabbed her arms and twisted her under him.

"Stop, stay down, Nikki!" He growled and gasped as her fingernails found the soft skin of the underside of his forearm.

"Quinn?" She gulped out his name as she struggled to breathe through her panic.

Noise burst all around. She heard gunfire from multiple directions, followed by shouts. Leaves and twigs crunched and snapped as men charged out from the trees, and she became aware that she and John, and Tim, had not been alone in the woods. As Quinn continued to hold her down, she felt his grip become softer. He hadn't tackled her to stop her, but to protect her, from the bullet that had been fired in her direction.

"It's okay, Nikki, I've got you." Quinn continued to hover over her, until he heard someone shout.

"All clear!"

Hesitantly, Quinn stood up, though he continued to keep his body between her and the two men that had been cuffed on the ground.

"Are you okay? Are you hurt?" Quinn gazed down at her, and offered his hand to help her up.

"I think I'm okay." Nikki eased herself to her knees, then took his hand. Her body ached, and she knew there were a few solid bruises scattered across her arms and legs from the car accident, and the rough way that Tim grabbed her. "Are you?" She got to her feet with a soft tug from him. She reached up and swept her fingertip through a trail of blood that ran from his temple.

"Yes, I'm fine." Quinn caught her hand with his free one. "It was just a branch I scratched myself on." His eyes were heavy with worry as they sought hers. "Are you sure you're okay? I'm sorry, I should have intervened sooner."

"Sooner?" She blinked as her heart skipped a beat. "How long were you there?"

"We followed John's car. But we had to wait for the right moment to announce our presence. Tim had his gun on you for so long, we didn't have a clear shot to take him out." He gazed at her, his eyes a bit wild as he looked her over from head to toe. "When I saw you run, I didn't know what would happen. I saw John aim at you, and I just did the first thing I could think to do."

"It was the right thing to do." Nikki squeezed his hands, then caught sight of a bullet hole in the tree right beside her. Her stomach churned at the thought of how close it came to striking her. "You saved my life, Quinn. Again." She smiled at the thought.

"You saved it." He brushed her hair back from her shoulders as he surveyed the state of her neck and shoulders. "Are you sure you weren't hurt? That crash by the police station sounded so loud."

"I'm fine." Nikki nodded, though her neck did feel a little sore. "You know about the crash?"

"Yes, I was at the station, I heard it. The car matched the description of the car in the surveillance video. That's when I called you, to update you that it wasn't Heather, and when you didn't answer, I started to worry. The police officer that chased after the car reported back that there was a male driver and female passenger, and all of a sudden I just knew." He shook his head. "I couldn't be sure, I followed my hunch."

"But I don't understand." Nikki frowned as she watched John and Tim escorted to two separate police cars. "You were here the whole time? You followed us? But I thought he lost the police car?" She felt a rush of fear as she recalled the reckless way that Tim drove through Dahlia.

"I instructed the officer to make it seem like he'd lost you. I didn't want to risk a high-speed chase that could end up in a collision. Once I believed you were inside of that car, all I wanted to do was get you back safe. If you hadn't crashed the car and gotten our attention, I'm not sure I ever would have found you." He cleared his throat, then lowered his eyes. "Maybe I made the wrong choices. Maybe I should have found a way to stop him sooner."

"You did the right thing." Nikki met his eyes. "Tim was so upset after the crash. I think if he felt any more pressure he would have shot me right there in the car." As she recalled their conversation, her own words echoed through her mind. Suddenly, her face flushed. Had Quinn heard what she said when she was pleading for her life? Did he hear her confession about being in love? Would he know that it was about him? As grateful as she was to be alive, in that moment she wished she could melt into the dirt beneath her feet.

"I don't want to even think about that." Quinn winced as he glanced away from her for a moment. "How did you end up in that car with him, Nikki?" When he looked back at her she saw a hint of frustration in his expression. "Why would you take a chance like that?"

"You mean Mrs. Whitter didn't call you?" Nikki's eyes widened as she suddenly realized that she had no idea if Mrs. Whitter was safe. "Did you go to her house?"

"Mrs. Whitter's house?" Quinn raised an eyebrow. "Why would we go there? I had no idea you were in any trouble until I suspected you were in that car. Now that we have John's confession we'll be able to arrest him for Bryan's murder, and I will make sure that Tim goes away for a long time for what he did to you." He reached up as if he might touch her cheek, but let his hand fall away instead.

"Oh no!" Nikki gasped, too distracted by Mrs. Whitter's safety to notice his hesitation. "We have to get to Mrs. Whitter right now! John said he was going back there to search the house. She's in danger!"

"What do you mean, why is she in danger?" Quinn followed after her as she ran towards the nearest patrol car. "Nikki?"

"There's no time, Quinn, I have to get there!" Nikki started to climb into the driver's seat of the police car. She didn't even think about what she was doing until Quinn caught her by the arm.

"Come with me, my car is right over here." Quinn steered her in the direction of it. Once they were settled in the car, he looked over at her. "Now, can you please tell me what happened?"

"Just drive, Quinn, please! She and Princess are all alone there, I hope he didn't hurt them." She wrung her hands as he started the car. "Hurry, please!"

"I'm hurrying." He flicked on the siren, threw his car into drive and the engine roared as he headed down the dirt road. "But you have to tell me the truth, Nikki, how did you end up in the car with Tim?" He glanced over at her, his eyes hot with a mixture of emotions.

"It wasn't by choice!" Nikki grabbed his phone from the middle console and opened it up. "I need to call my cell phone, I need to see if I can reach her."

"The password is 5798." He frowned as he concentrated on the road.

"Thank you!" Nikki typed in the password then began to dial her cell phone. It went straight to voicemail without ringing. She tried again, and it went to voicemail again. Her heart sank lower and lower as she left a message for Mrs. Whitter to call her. With a trembling finger she tried Mrs. Whitter's phone and it just rang. "My phone is going to voicemail. It must be off." She blinked back tears. "Oh no, something terrible must have happened."

Finally, she spilled the entire day's events to Quinn, including the location of the emeralds.

"Oh Nikki, I'm so sorry. I wish I would have known." He turned down the road that led to Mrs. Whitter's house.

"I never should have left her there alone." Nikki

wiped at her eyes as her muscles ached with the desire to jump out of the car and get to the house faster.

"You did the right thing." Quinn parked the car in front of the house, then grabbed her hand before she could leap out of the car. "Nikki, let me go in first."

"No!" She jerked her hand out of his grasp. "I need to see if she's okay for myself!"

As tears blurred Nikki's vision she ran for the front door.

"Mrs. Whitter!" She pushed the door open and headed straight for the laundry room. "Mrs. Whitter?" She gasped out her name as she pushed the chair away and grabbed for the handle of the door. The first thing she heard was a bark. Princess barked louder as Nikki fiddled with the lock to get the door open. "I'm here, Princess, I'm here, sweetie."

"Nikki, here let me." Quinn pushed her shaking hands away from the stubborn lock. With one swift twist he had the door open. He stepped back to allow Nikki to barrel through the door.

"Mrs. Whitter!" Nikki sighed with relief as she saw Mrs. Whitter near the back of the laundry room with Princess in her arms.

"Is it safe, dear?" Mrs. Whitter patted the top of the dog's head.

"It's safe." Nikki smiled as tears spilled down her cheeks. "Are you okay?"

"I'm fine, dear." Mrs. Whitter smiled, glanced at Quinn, then back at her. "Nothing to be too concerned about. I would like to get out of this laundry room, though." She held Nikki's phone out to her. "I figured out your plan, but unfortunately there is no service in this room. I am so sorry, Nikki. I know you were counting on me to be able to get you help."

"All I care about is that you are safe, Mrs. Whitter." Nikki stepped aside to let her out of the laundry room.

"You too, dear." Mrs. Whitter paused beside Nikki, then wrapped her arms around her, with Princess between them. The dog eagerly licked Nikki's cheeks. "I was so worried about you. You were so brave to stand up for me like that. Brave, and plain stupid!"

"Mrs. Whitter!" Nikki laughed, then shook her head. "I would do it again in a second."

"I should hope not." Mrs. Whitter raised her eyebrows. "You are young, and vibrant, and you have an entire life ahead of you. It's foolish to risk it for an old woman like me."

"Mrs. Whitter, you'll never be old, and you're one of my very best friends." Nikki hugged her again. "I would do absolutely anything to make sure that you're safe."

Princess gave a sharp bark.

"Yes, and you, too." Nikki grinned and kissed the top of the dog's head. "Happy birthday, Princess!"

"Well, then." Mrs. Whitter wiped quickly at her eyes to hide the tears that threatened to fall. "I suppose we can be done with all of that unpleasantness."

"Thanks to Quinn. If he hadn't shown up when he did—" Nikki trailed off as fresh fear rushed through her.

"The important thing is everyone is safe." Quinn wrapped one arm around her shoulders, then looked into her eyes.

"Yes, it is." She cleared her throat as she recalled the confession she'd made. Would Quinn know it was about him. She still had no idea if he had heard it. Part of her wanted him to tell her if he did, but a bigger part wanted him to pretend he hadn't heard a word.

"Oh my, the guests will be here any minute!" Mrs. Whitter set Princess down on the floor. "And that rotten criminal has made a mess of this place."

"Don't worry, Mrs. Whitter, we'll get it shaped up in no time." Nikki tipped her head in Quinn's direction. "Right, Quinn?"

"Well, I'm afraid this area will have to be investigated as a crime scene. We'll need to take custody of the emeralds as well." Quinn frowned. "I'm sorry, Mrs. Whitter, the party may have to be delayed."

"Nonsense!" Mrs. Whitter gasped. "It's Princess' birthday. The party must go on!"

"What if everyone stays outside?" Nikki looked over at Quinn. "That would work, wouldn't it?"

"I suppose." Quinn rubbed the back of his neck, then smiled. "Sure, I don't see why not."

"Great!" Nikki looped her arm around Mrs. Whitter's. "Let's get everything set up."

As Nikki headed out the door with the agility set under one arm and Mrs. Whitter's arm wrapped around the other, she paused and glanced back at Quinn. He stared in her direction, as if he'd yet to take his eyes off her. As she met his gaze, her heartbeat quickened. He smiled, and for an instant she was certain that he'd heard every word of her confession.

"Nikki, if we hurry we can still pick up Princess' balloons." Mrs. Whitter gave her arm a light tug.

"Oh yes, I can do that." Nikki looked away from Quinn, as her heart continued to race. "I need to check in on my other dogs, too, and at least give them potty breaks. Don't worry, Princess is going to have the best birthday party ever." She pushed the door closed behind her. Whether or not Quinn had heard her, the party had to go on.

The End

ALSO BY CINDY BELL

WAGGING TAIL COZY MYSTERIES

Murder at Pooch Park

SAGE GARDENS COZY MYSTERIES

Birthdays Can Be Deadly

Money Can Be Deadly

Trust Can Be Deadly

Ties Can Be Deadly

Rocks Can Be Deadly

Jewelry Can Be Deadly

Numbers Can Be Deadly

Memories Can Be Deadly

Paintings Can Be Deadly

Snow Can Be Deadly

Tea Can Be Deadly

Greed Can Be Deadly

DUNE HOUSE COZY MYSTERIES

Seaside Secrets

Boats and Bad Guys

Treasured History

Hidden Hideaways

Dodgy Dealings

Suspects and Surprises

Ruffled Feathers

A Fishy Discovery

Danger in the Depths

Celebrities and Chaos

Pups, Pilots and Peril

Tides, Trails and Trouble

Racing and Robberies

Athletes and Alibis

CHOCOLATE CENTERED COZY MYSTERIES

The Sweet Smell of Murder

A Deadly Delicious Delivery

A Bitter Sweet Murder

A Treacherous Tasty Trail

Pastry and Peril

Trouble and Treats

Fudge Films and Felonies

Custom-Made Murder

Skydiving, Soufflés and Sabotage

Christmas Chocolates and Crimes

Hot Chocolate and Homicide

Chocolate Caramels and Conmen

Picnics, Pies and Lies

DONUT TRUCK COZY MYSTERIES

Deadly Deals and Donuts

Fatal Festive Donuts

Bunny Donuts and a Body

BEKKI THE BEAUTICIAN COZY MYSTERIES

Hairspray and Homicide

A Dyed Blonde and a Dead Body

Mascara and Murder

Pageant and Poison

Conditioner and a Corpse

Mistletoe, Makeup and Murder

Hairpin, Hair Dryer and Homicide

Blush, a Bride and a Body

Shampoo and a Stiff

Cosmetics, a Cruise and a Killer

Lipstick, a Long Iron and Lifeless

Camping, Concealer and Criminals

Treated and Dyed

A Wrinkle-Free Murder

A MACARON PATISSERIE COZY MYSTERY SERIES

Sifting for Suspects

Recipes and Revenge

Mansions, Macarons and Murder

NUTS ABOUT NUTS COZY MYSTERIES

A Tough Case to Crack

A Seed of Doubt

Roasted Penuts and Peril

HEAVENLY HIGHLAND INN COZY MYSTERIES

Murdering the Roses

Dead in the Daisies

Killing the Carnations

Drowning the Daffodils

Suffocating the Sunflowers

Books, Bullets and Blooms

A Deadly Serious Gardening Contest

A Bridal Bouquet and a Body

Digging for Dirt

WENDY THE WEDDING PLANNER COZY MYSTERIES

Matrimony, Money and Murder

Chefs, Ceremonies and Crimes

Knives and Nuptials

Mice, Marriage and Murder

ABOUT THE AUTHOR

Cindy Bell is a USA Today and Wall Street Journal Bestselling Author. She is the author of the cozy mystery series Wagging Tail, Donut Truck, Dune House, Sage Gardens, Chocolate Centered, Macaron Patisserie, Nuts about Nuts, Bekki the Beautician, Heavenly Highland Inn and Wendy the Wedding Planner.

Cindy has always loved reading, but it is only recently that she has discovered her passion for writing romantic cozy mysteries. She loves walking along the beach thinking of the next adventure her characters can embark on.

You can sign up for her newsletter so you are notified of her latest releases at http://www.cindybellbooks.com.

Printed in Great Britain
by Amazon

24832560R00116